I0600655

Widow's Weeds

or

For Years I Couldn't Wear My Black

A Play in Three Acts

by Anthony Shaffer

A SAMUEL FRENCH ACTING EDITION

SAMUEL
FRENCH
FOUNDED 1830

SAMUELFRENCH.COM

Copyright © 1989 by Anthony Shaffer

ALL RIGHTS RESERVED

CAUTION: Professionals and amateurs are hereby warned that *WIDOW'S WEEDS* is subject to a Licensing Fee. It is fully protected under the copyright laws of the United States of America, the British Commonwealth, including Canada, and all other countries of the Copyright Union. All rights, including professional, amateur, motion picture, recitation, lecturing, public reading, radio broadcasting, television and the rights of translation into foreign languages are strictly reserved. In its present form the play is dedicated to the reading public only.

The amateur live stage performance rights to *WIDOW'S WEEDS* are controlled exclusively by Samuel French, Inc., and licensing arrangements and performance licenses must be secured well in advance of presentation. PLEASE NOTE that amateur Licensing Fees are set upon application in accordance with your producing circumstances. When applying for a licensing quotation and a performance license please give us the number of performances intended, dates of production, your seating capacity and admission fee. Licensing Fees are payable one week before the opening performance of the play to Samuel French, Inc., at 45 W. 25th Street, New York, NY 10010.

Licensing Fee of the required amount must be paid whether the play is presented for charity or gain and whether or not admission is charged.

Stock licensing fees quoted upon application to Samuel French, Inc.

For all other rights than those stipulated above, apply to: Peters Fraser & Dunlop, Drury House, 34-43 Russell Street, London WC2B 5HA, England.

Particular emphasis is laid on the question of amateur or professional readings, permission and terms for which must be secured in writing from Samuel French, Inc.

Copying from this book in whole or in part is strictly forbidden by law, and the right of performance is not transferable.

Whenever the play is produced the following notice must appear on all programs, printing and advertising for the play: "Produced by special arrangement with Samuel French, Inc."

Due authorship credit must be given on all programs, printing and advertising for the play.

ISBN   978-0-573-69080-8   Printed   in   U.S.A.   #25132

No one shall commit or authorize any act or omission by which the copyright of, or the right to copyright, this play may be impaired.

No one shall make any changes in this play for the purpose of production.

Publication of this play does not imply availability for performance. Both amateurs and professionals considering a production are strongly advised in their own interests to apply to Samuel French, Inc., for written permission before starting rehearsals, advertising, or booking a theatre.

No part of this book may be reproduced, stored in a retrieval system, or transmitted in any form, by any means, now known or yet to be invented, including mechanical, electronic, photocopying, recording, videotaping, or otherwise, without the prior written permission of the publisher.

MUSIC USE NOTE

Licensees are solely responsible for obtaining formal written permission from copyright owners to use copyrighted music in the performance of this play and are strongly cautioned to do so. If no such permission is obtained by the licensee, then the licensee must use only original music that the licensee owns and controls. Licensees are solely responsible and liable for all music clearances and shall indemnify the copyright owners of the play and their licensing agent, Samuel French, Inc., against any costs, expenses, losses and liabilities arising from the use of music by licensees.

IMPORTANT BILLING AND CREDIT
REQUIREMENTS

All producers of *WIDOW'S WEEDS must* give credit to the Author of the Play in all programs distributed in connection with performances of the Play, and in all instances in which the title of the Play appears for the purposes of advertising, publicizing or otherwise exploiting the Play and/or a production. The name of the Author *must* appear on a separate line on which no other name appears, immediately following the title and *must* appear in size of type not less than fifty percent of the size of the title type.

The premiere of WIDOW'S WEEDS was at Brewhouse Theatre, Taunton, England, on August 24, 1987, under the auspices of Gallery Productions, with the following cast:

Mrs. Florence Collier. . . . . Susan Hanson

Claire Parker. . . . . Joanne Good

Dick Richards. . . . . Christopher Strauli

Alex . . . . Michael Sherwin

Bernie . . . . Jason Salkey

Joe. . . . . Matthew Tinker

Philip Charles . . . . Adrian Mills

Reginald. . . . . Gian Sammarco

Christine. . . . . Lisa Geoghan

Mr. Younghusband. . . . . Derek Beard

Bill . . . . Shaun Curry

CAST IN ORDER OF APPEARANCE

MRS. FLORENCE COLLIER . . . . Housewife

CLAIRE PARKER . . . . Assistant to Philip Charles

DICK RICHARDS . . . . Film Director

ALEX . . . . Lighting Cameraman

BERNIE . . . . Grips

JOE . . . . Sound Man

PHILIP CHARLES . . . . Agency Producer

REGINALD . . . . Mrs. Collier's Son

CHRISTINE . . . . Mrs. Collier's Daughter

MR. YOUNGHUSBAND . . . . The Agency's Client

BILL . . . . A visitor to the house

N.B.

It may be found extremely advantageous to add the non-speaking part of an electrician to assist Alex with the lighting set ups and many clapperboard incidents. Like many such persons he should be large, hairy, and almost nude.

SETTING

The action of the play takes place in Mrs. Collier's living-room in Plaistow, London. Between mid-afternoon and dark. The action of the play, which is in three acts, is continuous.

WIDOW'S WEEDS
ACT I

"Home Sweet Home" — *Melba.*

SCENE: The curtain rises on the livingroom of MRS. COLLIER's house. The income group is lower middle class. It is neat, comfortable and clean, with the mass-produced furniture looking almost painfully spick and span. A three-piece suite occupies stage center. Stage right is a tiled fireplace in which burns an electric log fire. Stage left a door leads to a small hallway from where a door leads out to the street. Upstage center a door leads into a kitchen. Upstage left a staircase is in view leading off the hall to the upstairs rooms.

AT RISE: MRS. FLORENCE COLLIER, a woman of about 36, stands in front of the mirror above the mantelpiece making-up. On her cheeks are two red spots which she has put there inexpertly to disguise sallowness. She seems nervous and flustered and keeps glancing at the old-fashioned clock on the sideboard which shows 2:45. She breaks off to tidy what is already tidy, returning to the mirror to fiddle with her appearance.

The front DOORBELL rings and she moves quickly upstage to answer it. CLAIRE PARKER, a neat, pretty, efficient, fashionable girl of 23, stands on the threshold.

CLAIRE. *(cheerily)* Good afternoon, Mrs. Collier.

MRS. COLLIER. *(guarded)* Afternoon.

CLAIRE. You remember me? Claire Parker ... from Wren and Wiltshire ... You know, the Advertising Agency ... You *were* expecting us?

MRS. COLLIER. Yes, of course. Won't you come in, Miss Parker? I haven't been able to think of nothing else for days. Please do come in. (CLAIRE comes into the room. MRS. COLLIER closes the door and laughs.) I thought the twentieth would never come.

CLAIRE. Mrs. Collier, surely you aren't nervous?

MRS. COLLIER. *(a giggle)* Well just a little. You see, I've never done nothing like this before.

CLAIRE. Mrs. Collier, I assure you there's absolutely nothing to worry about. It's all quite straight-forward.

MRS. COLLIER. *(doubtful)* Well maybe for some.

CLAIRE. For everybody. We've done quite a few of them you know.

MRS. COLLIER. I suppose you must 'ave.

CLAIRE. Yes. Lots of them. And all our ladies have been really super. In fact the one we had yesterday practically begged us to come back and do her again today.

MRS. COLLIER. Oh, she was having you on.

CLAIRE. Absolutely not. Mrs. Paton — that's the name of the lady we shot — wouldn't do a thing like that.

MRS. COLLIER. The lady you what?

CLAIRE. Shot! — you know ... filmed. She wasn't having us on at all. She enjoyed every minute of it. And so will you.

MRS. COLLIER. Oh I dunno about that. I don't mind telling you Miss Parker, I've fair got the collywobbles.

Really I have.

CLAIRE. Come now, Mrs. Collier, you mustn't worry. All you've got to do is sit down, say your piece, and it'll all be over in no time. It's rather like going to the dentist. One worries and worries and worries, and finally one gets there, and it turns out to be some dreamy daddsy figure giving you the old one-two with his steady professional eyes, and telling you *(deep grave voice)* "this might hurt you just for a moment or two, but if it gets too much, just tell me, dear lady." And of course one doesn't argue. One just lies back and enjoys it.

MRS. COLLIER. That's as may be. My dentist's a nineteen-year-old medical student down at the General. "To be frank with you, Mrs. Collier," he says, "To be frank, I've never pulled a tooth before." "Well, mate" I says to him, "I haven't got no spares for you to practice on. So hop it."

CLAIRE. All I really mean to say is that there's nothing to worry about.

MRS. COLLIER. I suppose not. *(MRS. COLLIER goes back to the mirror and starts to fiddle with her hair. CLAIRE watches her, conscious that she has done little to put her at ease.)*

CLAIRE. *(kindly)* The others won't be long. Shall we have a cup of tea while we wait for them to get here.

MRS. COLLIER. I'll make it now. I've got the kettle on. *(MRS. COLLIER goes out through the door to the kitchen. CLAIRE inspects the room, wandering about, picking up objects for close scrutiny, and peering at the wall decorations, one of which is the top of a large chocolate box showing a white, beamed cottage set in a riotous flower garden. She does all this with a slightly superior air to indicate that the furnishings are "not her.")*

CLAIRE. *(calling)* This is a nice room. You've done it up very prettily. It's so homely.

MRS. COLLIER. *(calling from the kitchen)* Oh do you really think so? *(CLAIRE holds up a cheap china figure of a shepherdess, grimaces and replaces it.)*

CLAIRE. Absolutely. It's quite obvious that you've taken the most awful trouble with it.

MRS. COLLIER. *(calling, pleased)* Do you really think so?

CLAIRE. Yes. You can tell it's a real home alright. Everything used and cozy and familiar. Home is where you hang yourself.

MRS. COLLIER. What's that dear?

CLAIRE. *(She peers closely at "home-sweet-home" sampler on the wall.)* Everyone's going to be very pleased with it. It's super for TV.

MRS. COLLIER. *(calling)* Well it's better that that there contemporary stuff with all the spiky legs. My friend Mrs. Barber's got some of it. It's like being in a room with great big beetles. You think, when you put the light out, they are going to come for you. *(CLAIRE laughs and looks at the solid legs of the furniture.*

CLAIRE. No fear of that here.

(MRS. COLLIER Enters with the tea tray which she sets down on a table.)

MRS. COLLIER. What's that?

CLAIRE. Things walking about in the dark.

MRS. COLLIER. *(suddenly uneasy)* What do you mean? Why should they?

CLAIRE. I was talking about the furniture. I mean it's pretty solid.

MRS. COLLIER. I see. *(MRS. COLLIER starts to pour the tea in silence.)* Sugar?

CLAIRE. I'd love to but not at my fighting weight. *(CLAIRE takes a bottle of saccharine out of her bag and puts two in the tea. They drink in silence.)*

MRS. COLLIER. I do hope I'll do alright.

CLAIRE. Now you're not to start worrying about that again. I've told you there's nothing to it. My boss — that's Philip Charles — will do the interviewing. *(CLAIRE puts down her tea to demonstrate.)*

CLAIRE. He'll plonk himself down here and just ask you to go through your story — you know, the one you told the research lady who first visited you.

MRS. COLLIER. What, the one with the stutter? Mrs. Rogers?

CLAIRE. Yes. That's her.

MRS. COLLIER. I liked her. You can trust people what's got infirmities.

CLAIRE. After you've told your story, Mr. Charles will ask you a few questions arising out of it, and that'll be all.

MRS. COLLIER. I'm so excited. I really am ... Tell me, Miss Parker, how exactly did you come to choose me? I mean, I'm not the sort of person as whatever wins pools, and premium bonds and things.

CLAIRE. Please call me Claire.

MRS. COLLIER. Alright — But Claire, how did they come to pick me?

CLAIRE. Wren and Wiltshire have a research department who employ people to go around asking house-wives how they came to use the shampoo. If their story is good, that is to say has good recall value, and the product genuinely did for them what they say it did, then they are selected and I call on them to see if they'd like to appear on television.

MRS. COLLIER. I'll bet none of them don't refuse.

CLAIRE. It's like the second coming. Some of them simply aren't photogenic and we can't use them.

MRS. COLLIER. *(in alarm)* Photogenic?

CLAIRE. Don't look good on the tele. We at Wren and Wilstshire don't believe that ugliness is the first blessed step to self-knowledge. Our beauty advisers seem to think it's all a matter of bone structure and castor oil.

MRS. COLLIER. Castor oil...

CLAIRE. One brimming tablespoon a day rubbed well in brings out the bloom on the skin.

MRS. COLLIER. Oh we don't use it for that in this household.

CLAIRE. No. Well I daresay it *has* got other uses. Actually I've got a girl friend who rubs a half-pound tin of cat food into her face every evening. She thinks the thiamin will bring out what she calls her "natural luster." Poor deluded cow! All that happens is that the acne pops out like mushrooms after rain.

MRS. COLLIER. Well you can't tell people can you? *(MRS. COLLIER looks at herself in the mirror.)* You've prob-ably noticed. I've left my eyes. I thought perhaps the Cleopatra look would suit.

CLAIRE. *(cheerful but firm)* Just leave the make-up to me, Mrs. Collier. I'll make you look super. Don't you worry.

(CLAIRE gets up and starts to ramble around the room.)

Mrs. Collier. Do you do the make-up as well then?

Claire. I did it for a year before I went to the agency. And what's more, I've got a union ticket to prove it.

Mrs. Collier. *(suddenly envious)* You've done quite a lot in your life, ain't you, Claire?

Claire. *(sober)* Not so much ... A little better than par for the course. *(CLAIRE comes across a photograph of MRS. COLLIER'S children which she picks up.)* Are these your children? *(MRS. COLLIER is suddenly nervous. She takes the photograph away from CLAIRE with more force than necessary.*

Mrs. Collier. Yes, Reginald and Christine. *(She puts the photograph face downwards on the sideboard.)*

Claire. *(puzzled)* How old are they?

Mrs. Collier. *(abstracted)* I don't know.

Claire. You *don't know?*

Mrs. Collier. *(with an effort)* Reginald is fifteen. The girl's a year younger.

Claire. How lucky to have them the right way round.

Mrs. Collier. *(heavily)* Lucky?

Claire. Absolutely. Really super clever. You know — the boy before the girl. *(MRS. COLLIER nods defensively.)* I suppose they're at school now?

Mrs. Collier. Eh?

Claire. The kids.

Mrs. Collier. *(decisively)* Yes. That's right. They won't be back for hours.

Claire. Oh dear! I was rather hoping we could pop

them in the commercial.

MRS. COLLIER. *(very alarmed)* In the commercial? ... Oh no. That's quite impossible ... out of the question.

CLAIRE. But Mrs. Collier we've found that children are a must in these family commericals. After all we are selling to mothers.

MRS. COLLIER. No, no. I won't have them interviewed. I ... I won't have them badgered with no questions.

CLAIRE. But Mrs. Collier, I assure you there's no question of their being badgered or anything like that. Philip Charles is the most tactful and experienced...

MRS. COLLIER. No, I'm afraid not. This is something I cannot allow.

CLAIRE. I can understand your concern for the children of course, but surely you must realize...

MRS. COLLIER. *(very distressed, shouting)* No! Do you understand? I will not have it. For the last time — no!

(The two women look at each other in surprise at the sudden violence. The DOORBELL chimes. With a shrug CLAIRE goes to open it. On the threshold stands DICK RICHARDS, the film's director. He's a rather obviously paradoxical man, fat and energetic; sensitive, cheerful and melancholy — a young old man who finds himself, at 36, a professional in the wrong profession.)

DICK. Afternoon, Claire. And you'll be Mrs. Collier. *(MRS. COLLIER is still under a spell.)*

MRS. COLLIER. Eh? Oh yes. That's me.

DICK. My name's Dick Richards. I'm directing the film this afternoon.

MRS. COLLIER. It won't take long? I hope it won't take long.

DICK. We'll be through in no time. *(to CLAIRE:)* We're getting quite expert at these interviews now, aren't we Claire? *(to MRS. COLLIER:)* The set up will be relatively simple and all we shall need apart, that is, from yourself, is a couple of cutaway shots of...

CLAIRE. *(hurriedly)* Mrs. Collier was just telling me about her children. She doesn't want them in the shot.

MRS. COLLIER. It's not right to question them. Besides, they won't be home.

DICK. It's a pity. But if they won't be home, that's it. But perhaps your husband would...

MRS. COLLIER. *(touch of hysteria)* I'm alone here. All alone.

DICK. *(pacifying)* I see. Well it doesn't really matter. After all, you're our star, Mrs. Collier. *(She relaxes slightly and half smiles. CLAIRE closes the door while DICK advances into the room, taking off his old camel-haired "location" coat and looking about him.)* Ah tea! Just what I want.

MRS. COLLIER. Would you like some? I'll get you a cup.

DICK. Please don't trouble yourself for my sake, Mrs. Collier.

MRS. COLLIER. It's no trouble for *you,* Mr. Richards. *(MRS. COLLIER goes into the kitchen. A slight pause ensues while DICK takes stock.)*

DICK. Claire, darling, I don't want to be bitchy, but I've always understood your function in this carnival as being i/c oil, troubled water for the pouring on.

CLAIRE. Well you're wrong. I've changed my job. I'm now i/c cat, pigeons for the putting amongst.

DICK. Oh we are sharp this afternoon. But I'm quite

serious. I thought your job was to set our artistes at ease; to present to the suspicious and malevolent Mrs. Corgi here for instance...

CLAIRE. Mrs. Collier.

DICK. Mrs. Collier, a picture of ourselves as lovable old uncles and aunties from the Arts Council who somehow seem to have strayed for the afternoon into the distasteful world of commerce. Instead of which you've apparently convinced her that we're child rapists.

CLAIRE. I know. I can't understand it.

DICK. I can, quite easily ... You rushed in here, forgot you were not in your own little barnyard in Chelsea, and gave her a steady stream of Mumsy — and — Mary — Quant. It's not surprising she's pissed off.

CLAIRE. Honestly it's not my fault. I was perfectly super to her. In fact, we were getting along jolly well until I saw the photo of the kids. Then she started. Got quite hysterical. *(DICK picks up the photograph and examines it.)*

DICK. H'm, they look normal enough. The usual love affair with carbohydrates.

CLAIRE. You should talk. It's not for nothing you're known as Moby Dick Richards — the great white whale of Twickenham.

DICK. Incivility in you, my dear Claire, is not just a simple vice of the soul, it is the effect of several vices, namely Ignorance of Duty, Contempt for Others, Immoderate Pride and Ungovernable Jealousy.

CLAIRE. Jealousy?

DICK. Yes. Of one older and grosser than yourself. *(CLAIRE puts her hand on DICK'S arm in the gesture of sudden affection.)*

CLAIRE. *(suddenly sincere)* I'm not jealous of you, Dick...
I never was. *(They look at each other for a moment remembering
another time.)*

DICK. Don't you think I don't know that? What would
I have that anyone should envy?

CLAIRE. Oh, Dick... Dick! If only you'd stop being so
defensive about what you do. So you're not Truffaut or
Bunuel. Who cares? You're a super bloke. You're kind
and funny. People get on with you. I could ... once. But
not now. Why not Dick? Why not now?

DICK. *(slowly)* I was younger then. It didn't matter not
being anyone special. You don't expect it, and somehow
it's rather cozy with the promise being all in the future,
and the golden days to come. But now I know, now I
know what it's all about. It's all about happy, smiling
families: Mum is smilingly concerned; dad is smilingly
responsible; the kids are smilingly mischievous, but locked
together in the Slough of Coyness — bright mirrors held
up to reflect the attitudes of brand managers on their best
behavior — frozen and stunted as the gnomes on their
lawns. "All that clients ever want is a happy smiling
family that everyone can identify with." And you know
something "I don't know any."

CLAIRE. Isn't that rather your problem? Do you really
think all that stuff matters to me?

DICK. I don't suppose it does. But it matters to me. I
think it's the only thing that does these days.

CLAIRE. I suppose there's no way I can persuade you to
live happily ever after — with yourself.

DICK. Within my potential you mean? Within an area
circumscribed by consumer products? Don't worry

about it, my dear. My potential and I meet every morning in my shaving mirror, where we stare each other out. We've learnt to rub along quite jauntily together. Self disgust, you know, was never one of my more sustained vices.

CLAIRE. With a colossal ego like yours, sweetie, it really couldn't be.

DICK. Thank you. It's the same ego you used to find so fascinating.

CLAIRE. I still do. I just wish that *you* didn't. *(pause)* Sorry. I only meant for you to enjoy what you're good at — and allow someone else to enjoy it with you. That's all. I'm sorry about lousing this up though. Honest. *(DICK smiles at her with sudden tenderness.)*

DICK. Don't worry about it. I expect my shimmering charm will put all to rights. *(MRS. COLLIER comes in with teacup.)*

MRS. COLLIER. Here we are. How do you like it?

DICK. Strong please. Four lumps.

CLAIRE. That should read two. *(MRS. COLLIER smiles vaguely and passes the tea. She gives him four lumps.*

DICK. Thank you, Mrs. Collier. I don't suppose anyone has thought to tell you what exactly is going to happen here this afternoon.

MRS. COLLIER. Well, I know we're going to make a commercial for the telly.

DICK. True. But it's not quite as simple as that. In the film business we don't just set up our camera and shoot. The ceremony has to be attended by a horde of layabout acolytes mysteriously called grips, props, chippies and sparks — and it is their function to delay and confuse.

Mrs. Collier. Oh dear.

Dick. How right you are, Mrs. Collier, to say "oh dear." Even now, behind the front door, there is encamped just such an army, lounging against the generator, eating fried egg sandwiches, and waiting for an opportunity to sack your house.

Mrs. Collier. *(alarmed)* They did say they wouldn't make no mess.

Dick. Nor shall they. The union insists on their presence but only a fraction of them will be allowed in here, and the cleanest and neatest fraction at that. Alex Orton will light as well as operate the camera and I might say, I would trust him in Wedgewood's showroom. A solitary sound man, and what we call a grips, all, once again of impeccable daintiness, will complete the roster of the hired help; that is, of course, apart from Claire here who doubles as the make-up girl and will have you looking like a film star.

Mrs. Collier. Just so long as it's not Yul Brynner.

(The DOORBELL rings. MRS. COLLIER giggles as she goes to open it. BERNIE, the grips, Enters carrying dust sheets. He is a burly, middle-aged man, extremely competent at his work.)

Bernie. How do, Missus.

Mrs. Collier. Good afternoon.

(He starts to move furniture and lay the sheets. ALEX ORTON Enters carrying lights. He is the cameraman ... fiftyish, spry and jaunty and cheerfully efficient. Last to Enter is the sound man JOE with his lightweight "nagra" recording apparatus. As BERNIE

*works spreading the dust sheets, ALEX works to bring in the lights
and mount them — 5 ks, 2 ks, bashers and pups, onto their stands.
BERNIE then brings in the rails for the camera, then finally the
dolly and the camera itself — a blimped Mitchell. DICK selects an
armchair which he places upstage center left, facing 'the
audience.)*

DICK. Mrs. Collier, would you be so kind as to take
your seat in this armchair for a moment so we can start
getting a line-up?

MRS. COLLIER. What like this? *(MRS. COLLIER crosses to
pose haughtily in the armchair.)*

DICK. Just sit normally, Mrs. Collier. We are not
recording Her Majesty's Christmas Broadcast to the
nation. *(MRS. COLLIER relaxes as ALEX hands DICK a view-
finder and he proceeds to move around the room with it, trying to fix
the set-up in consultation with him.)* I think we'll keep it simple ... Make the back position about here. We'll go with a
75. Mrs. Collier just look at me for a moment, will you?
No, we'll go on a 50, and higher — from here. It's hair
we're after. And then a slow track in to about here, to lose
Philip and frame up on a big close up of Mrs. Collier.
Right?

ALEX. Philip will be where, exactly? *(DICK drags another
armchair into position opposite MRS. COLLIER.)*

DICK. Here.

ALEX. OK. Mrs. Collier can stand out now. *(DICK helps
MRS. COLLIER to her feet.)*

DICK. Who did your hair, Mrs. Collier? It's most
fetching.

MRS. COLLIER. *(suddenly nervous)* Er ... The Salon Pompadour. It's in the High Street. Glad you like it.

DICK.   Indeed I do. We shall move really close into it to frame every lustrous follicle. *(He gestures the frame with his hands, moving towards her. She back away hastily.)*

DICK.   Claire, would you start Mrs. Collier's make-up now, please? *(aside to CLAIRE:)* Do you think you might try and remove the atmosphere of the big top? *(CLAIRE grimaces at him and leads MRS. COLLIER stage right, where she sits her in a chair and gets down to work.)*

MRS. COLLIER.   It's a bit trickly this work, isn't it?

CLAIRE.   Not really. The most difficult thing I've ever had to do was to tattoo a snake on the stomach of a Turkish belly dancer with violent indigestion. It looked more like a centipede with fallen arches. *(The lamps are being erected on their stands by ALEX. BERNIE joins up the rail section and secures them with wooden wedges. He then runs the dolly up and down to see the ride is smooth.)*

DICK.   Has anyone seen Philip Charles?

BERNIE.   *(Welsh accent)* He's outside in his car, sir. He said he wanted to be alone till we was ready.

DICK.   I'd have thought that Garbo routine would look a bit ridiculous in the back of an Austin Princess.

(PHILIP CHARLES, the Agency producer, Enters through the chaos. He's blond, thin and suave in the stilted manner of a man coming from a poor family who has learnt his manners from books. He is desperately ambitious, clever, hard-working, and would stand up his girl friend if it meant 10 minutes with the chairman of the board. He wears a neat business suit of exaggerated cut. The tie is floral and unrestrained.)

PHILIP. Did I hear my name taken in vain?

DICK. Hullo Philip. We'd given you up.

PHILIP. I was sitting in the car doing my homework.
(He sees CLAIRE making up MRS. COLLIER.)

PHILIP. So that's our heroine. She looks O.K.

DICK. She'll be alright once your assistant has expunged the influence of Grock.

PHILIP. Any problems?

DICK. There's something about the kids. She doesn't want them to appear in the film.

PHILIP. What? Why not?

DICK. I don't know. They've probably got scales instead of skin. Why don't you ask Claire?

PHILIP. *(calling)* Claire. Could you spare us a minute?

CLAIRE. *(to MRS. COLLIER:)* Won't be a sec. *(She crosses to meet PHILIP.)* Hullo, Phil. I didn't see you arrive.

PHILIP. Ah! We see you. You don't always see us. What's all this I hear about Mrs. Collier and her kids?

CLAIRE. She doesn't want them to be in the spot. When I mentioned it she became quite hysterical.

DICK. Can't say I blame her really. Children are notorious scene stealers.

ALEX. *(to DICK:)* We're about ready for the talent, DICK.

DICK. Alright. Light them up. *(ALEX puts his head round the door and bellows to the unseen generator operator.)*

ALEX. Let's have them on!

(The LIGHTS come on one by one. DICK moves over to the camera.)

PHILIP. It's a familiar problem, Claire. We've met it before. We'll just have to persuade her.

CLAIRE. It wasn't just she didn't want them to appear in a commercial, Phil. It was something else. It was as if she was frightened for them, and was trying to protect them.

PHILIP. Frightened!.... Where are these children?

CLAIRE. At school.

PHILIP. All the afternoon?

CLAIRE. Well if she'd cooperate we might be able to get them released early. After all they don't do any actual work in the afternoons do they?

PHILIP. Don't they?

CLAIRE. Of course not. It's only forcible milk feeding or scout's knots, or something equally futile. I'm sure they'd much rather be making movies.

PHILIP. I'll have a word with her.

DICK. *(squinting through the camera)* Philip. Can we have you in please? *(PHILIP goes towards the camera.)*

PHILIP. Do I sit here?

DICK. Yes. *(PHILIP sits. DICK regards his position through the camera.)* Lean right back. That's right. Now cross your legs. Good. Claire, sit in for Mrs. Collier would you? *(CLAIRE crosses to sit in the other chair. To BERNIE:)* Ease out a fraction, Bernie. *(BERNIE pulls the camera back.)*

PHILIP. That's it!

DICK. That's it. Hold it there and mark it. Mrs. Collier, can we have you in now, please? *(MRS. COLLIER, now made-up, makes her way onto the "set" and takes her seat in her chair opposite PHILIP. DICK continues to study the set up, then gestures for the dolly to be pulled right back.)* That's your back *position. Alex, it's all yours. (ALEX now starts in earnest to light the set, taking frequent readings from his light meter and giving a steady stream of orders to "spot it up" or "put a wire in it", etc. to himself. BERNIE marks his position and pushes the dolly into various positions along the track and also works out the distances to the artists with his tape measure. This whole setting up process goes on ceaselessly during the next scene.)*

PHILIP. Hullo, Mrs. Collier. I'm Philip Charles — the Agency producer from Wren and Wiltshire. I wrote to you about all this a few weeks ago. Do you remember?

MRS. COLLIER. Oh yes. Pleased to meet you.

PHILIP. I'm the one who's going to be asking all the questions. I'll try and make it as painless as possible.

MRS. COLLIER. Course I done nothing like this before. *(She glances nervously about her — at the camera, and the busy electricians, and the lamps which dazzle her.)*

PHILIP. Oh we know that. This must all seem very strange to you.

MRS. COLLIER. *(with a laugh)* Well it's different to what I thought.

PHILIP. Yes. Most people don't realize what it takes to do even the simplest bit of filming. But don't let it worry you. All you've got to do is just relax and enjoy it.

MRS. COLLIER. It won't take long will it?

PHILIP. Not once we've got started. They're just finishing lighting at the moment.

MRS. COLLIER. I see. *(ALEX starts lighting MRS. COLLIER'S hair, they work fairly close to her and thus come between her and PHILIP making conversation difficult.)*

PHILIP. Mrs. Collier I wonder if you would mind if I just had a quick word with Claire while that is going on. I'd just like to check my notes.

MRS. COLLIER. Not at all. *(CLAIRE comes and kneels by the side of his chair. She hands him his file which he has placed on the floor. He leafs through it.)*

PHILIP. Now let's go through this once again. It wouldn't do to miss a point.

CLAIRE. *(drily)* We haven't done yet.

PHILIP. *(mock pompous)* Thanks to constant vigilance, Miss Parker. *(Reads rapidly.)* The five points to be adduced from housewives in Folliclean interviews are as follows. One. Regular use. Two. Efficiency. Three. Physical Properties and sensations. Four. Use by whole family. Five. Dandruff completely cleared and has not returned. Right. The list seems to stack up against Mrs. Collier's story pretty well. Now you say we are going to be in trouble, human-interest wise. Do you think money would help?

CLAIRE. It would get you everywhere with me.

PHILIP. Unfortunately for us, Mrs. Collier is not a hump-happy harlot like you, Claire, but a respectably married woman. What do you think is our best approach?

DICK. I should have thought it was pretty obvious. *(parody PHILIP)* Mrs. Collier, we wish to explore your innocent babes for gold. They will be required to appear playing furiously with their doll's house, or chemical set, or painting-by-numbers kit, or whatever, for a screen period not exceeding ten seconds. For this they will not only be paid a sum greatly exceeding the weekly wage of a coal miner on double overtime, but will also be immortalized on celluloid by the highly selective, pictorially faultless eye of Mr. Dick Richards, regiesseur extraordinaire.

PHILIP. Here we go again. People prostituted. Talent debauched. It's a shameful thing — the story of advertising. It's amazing how I manage to live with it.

DICK. You could live with Jack the Ripper.

PHILIP. Now, now. No hero worship if you please. But what really interests me is why you're so ashamed of what you do. Tell me, Dick, is it because you think you can do better work than commercials, or are afraid you can't? *(malicious)* After all, you can't expose yourself too much in thirty seconds, can you?

DICK. You've only got to spend half and hour in Hyde park to know the folly of that remark. *(DICK turns away and then swings back.)* I suppose you've got that client of yours coming this afternoon ... What's his name?

PHILIP. *(Looks defensive.)* Er...

DICK. You know — the Managing Director of Sanitized Industries.

PHILIP. You mean Lionel Younghusband.

DICK. Lionel Oldwife would be nearer the mark, judging by the tales he puts out about his products.

PHILIP. I hope he won't be, but he's in town so I expect he will. That's why I need those kids. You know how he is about "family feeling."

CLAIRE. *(northern accent)* It's no use flying in the face of human nature. Folks like to see kids.

PHILIP. Exactly. And it was your job to persuade Mrs. Collier to let us use them.

CLAIRE. I told you, she got hysterical whenever I mentioned them. There was nothing I could do.

DICK. Her maternal instinct probably told her that they'd be exposed to Lionel Younghusband. You can't blame her for trying to protect them.

PHILIP. Oh come on now. He's not so bad.

DICK. He makes me nervous.

PHILIP. Nervous?

DICK. He's not concerned at all with what I do.

PHILIP. Are you concerned with what he does?

DICK. I don't employ him.

PHILIP. So where's your sense of duty? You wouldn't care if your commerical didn't sell one bottle of Folliclean, provided it was a super film. You can't expect him to respect you.

DICK. Why not? He owes me the respect commerce owes to art.

PHILIP. You really do love biting the hand that feeds you don't you? I'll tell you, if it wasn't for the Lionel Younghusbands of this world, you'd be out of work.

DICK. Oh for Christ's sake Philip don't give me that advertising — the new patron of the Arts routine.

PHILIP. And so it is.

DICK. Rubbish, that's like old Prince Lichnowsky going up to Beethoven and saying "Look here, Ludwig, this choral symphony's all very well for you long hairs, but I'm paying for it and I want you to write a few nice carols that people can sing."

CLAIRE. Smarty pants!

DICK. Don't you mean "clever Dick?" *(Shouts to ALEX.)* Hey, Alex, do you feel an aperture coming on?

ALEX. Nearly ready for you, Dick. Just a couple of minutes.

DICK. And what's more, he doesn't even pay you the respect commerce usually pays to commerce.

PHILIP. What's that supposed to mean?

DICK. Whenever he appears you do enough running, jumping and crawling through hoops to make the Olympic Decathalon team.

PHILIP. I've got an account to protect, that's all. I know he's difficult but so are most clients.

DICK. Difficult is one thing. Insane by reason of omniscience is another. Beats me why you want to hang on to the wretched account.

PHILIP. They spend nearly half a million with us, that's why, and if I didn't look after it, someone else would. Heaven knows it's rocky enough at the moment as it is.

DICK. And you mean, all it needs is for you to give up your well-known impersonation of Uriah Heep whenever he's around, for it to be off down the road.

PHILIP. Don't be such a smart-ass. There is a great difference between humoring a difficult client and playing Uriah Heep.

DICK. On the Toady Scale, the difference is hardly detectable.

PHILIP. As is the difference between your job and mine. I'm getting a little bored with this "artist-as-a-free-man" spiel of yours. You seem to forget that you too are in commerce — to be precise, in the business of making little films destined to persuade little people to buy little products. There is nothing dishonorable in this, or anything to be ashamed of, and if Lionel Younghusband's lack of sensibility bugs you so much, may I suggest that you have things all wrapped up before he gets here. *(DICK snaps off a mock salute.)*

DICK. Right you are, sir.

PHILIP. And do try and remember what I told you about this being a rocky account. If Mr. Younghusband does turn up this afternoon, I want you to toe the line.

DICK. *(military)* Sir! *(DICK does a smart about-turn and marches off to join ALEX and BERNIE. They start practicing tracking the camera in on DICK'S signal — a raised arm.)*

CLAIRE. He's super, really. It's a pity he's so damaged.

PHILIP. Damaged?

CLAIRE. Well you know — fractured. I suppose it doesn't really matter so long as his illusions protect him.

PHILIP. I'm afraid I'm only interested in how far his disillusions will protect me. He's becoming somewhat underemployable, is Mr. Richards.

CLAIRE. You don't want to take him to seriously.

PHILIP. I seldom do. But he said one interesting thing — when he mentioned exploiting the Collier kids for gold. I wonder if that's the answer.

CLAIRE. Not from where I'm sitting. However, if you want to stick your neck out, here's your big chance. *(ALEX having finished lighting MRS. COLLIER, clears the area between her and PHILIP leaving them face to face, sitting in their chairs. CLAIRE rises and moves stage right to pick her make-up things.)*

PHILIP. Hullo again, how do you feel now?

MRS. COLLIER. Not so bad, thank you.

PHILIP. I must say, Claire's done a marvellous make-up job on you. Have you seen yourself?

MRS. COLLIER. Yes. They've done me a treat. Even the kids wouldn't recognize me.

PHILIP. Ah the kids! I was just about to come to them.

MRS. COLLIER. *(sharply)* They're at school.

PHILIP. I know. But I was hoping that it might perhaps be possible to recall them early, so they could appear with you in the commercial. Of course you would be generously compensated for this interruption in their...

MRS. COLLIER. No. That's impossible. I've already told your assistant I just don't want to know about it — even for money. In fact I want you and all this lot out of here, by the time they come back.

PHILIP. But Mrs. Collier, surely you expected us here today?

MRS. COLLIER. That's as maybe. But I didn't expect all this crowd — such a fuss and bother.

PHILIP. I know. It must seem as if you've got a whole regiment in your house, but I assure you we are working with the smallest possible crew. Besides, I'd feel flattered if I were you. After all they're only all here because of you. I'll bet the neighbors aren't half green with envy. *(MRS. COLLIER looks mollified. Suddenly she giggles...)*

MRS. COLLIER. That Mrs. Baker at 34 will be going cross-eyed trying to look through her net curtains.

(The SOUND MAN approaches with two chest mikes.)

JOE. *(to PHILIP:)* If you'll just put this under your jacket, Mr. Charles? *(PHILIP slips it on.)* Thank you, sir. Now missus if you'll do likewise and conceal the instrument under your blouse.

MRS. COLLIER. *(suspicious)* 'ere what is it?

JOE. It's what we call a chest mike, my dear. It means you can say your piece and none of your beautiful face won't be hidden. Course I prefer a boom mike myself, but it's not having the room, see?

MRS. COLLIER. And you want me to put this under my blouse?

JOE. That's the idea, lady. Want me to give you a hand? *(He makes a move towards her. She starts back in the chair.)*

MRS. COLLIER. You've got a nerve, you 'ave. I'll stick that thing up you if you come near me.

JOE. Now look here, missus, I'm only trying to do my job. You don't want it to be in picture, do you? Come on. Let me give you a hand.

MRS. COLLIER. Not on your Nellie. I know your sort.

PHILIP. *(shouting)* Claire! *(CLAIRE moves over to them.)* Claire. Give Mrs. Collier a hand with her mike, will you? *(In an elaborate pantomime of modesty, CLAIRE conceals the microphone under MRS. COLLIER'S blouse. The sound man, JOE, returns grumbling, to his tape recorder. As he passes the camera crew BERNIE manages a sotto voce comment.)*

BERNIE. Fancied it a bit then, did yer?

JOE. It's all part of the service.

BERNIE. A man of your age — it's not natural.

DICK. Can we have a little hush, please?

ALEX. Keep it down lads.

DICK. *(to MRS. COLLIER:)* A₁ you quite happy with your mike, now Mrs. Collier?

MRS. COLLIER. *(with a giggle)* He might have warmed it up first.

DICK. That won't take long. Now all you have to do is to just speak normally. You don't have to raise your voice, or shout. Understand?

MRS. COLLIER. Oh, yes.

DICK. Now Mrs. Collier, I want you to listen very carefully to what I'm going to tell you because your entire performance depends on it. As you know, this commercial takes the form of an interview with Philip Charles the man sitting opposite you.

MRS. COLLIER. Right you are.

DICK. It's a very simple interview — in fact, all you have to do is to retell the story you first told to the research lady who called here — the story of how you first came to use Folliclean, and what it did for you and your family. O.K.?

MRS. COLLIER. You want me to tell the story just like I told 'er?

DICK. Precisely.

MRS. COLLIER. But where do I begin?

DICK. Leave all that to Philip here. He'll ask you the right questions and you'll find yourself telling the story without even noticing you're doing so. At the start he will ask you whether you and your family are regular users of Folliclean, and if the dandruff has ever returned. The answers to these two questions, let me hasten to remind you, are respectively yes and no.

PHILIP. Which, of course, is no more than the truth.

DICK. I am delighted to hear it. Now, Mrs. Collier, if you will just speak a few words so that our sound man can get a voice level. *(Shouts.)* Going for a sound level. *(JOE starts his machine.)*

MRS. COLLIER. *(Giggles.)* I can't think of nothing to say.

PHILIP. Perhaps I can assist. Mrs. Collier, are you a regular television viewer?

MRS. COLLIER. Oh yes. I don't like to miss the telly. It's a great comfort.

PHILIP. And what's your favorite programme?

MRS. COLLIER. "The Avengers." I think John Steed's so handsome. *(Laughs.)* So debonair — you know.

PHILIP. Yes. I think he's super.

JOE. OK for level.

DICK. Well then. Let battle commence. Philip?

PHILIP. Fine by me.

DICK. Mrs. Collier. Are you ready?

MRS. COLLIER. *(nervous)* I'm not sure ... Couldn't we wait a minute ... I mean...

DICK. Look, why don't we make a start? We can always stop and begin again.

MRS. COLLIER. *(dubious)* Alright...

DICK. Good. Now I've got three little rules I want you to remember as we go along. Listen carefully to the question you are asked. Don't ever look at the camera. And most important of all — behave naturally. As you would in everyday life. Don't try and act. It will just look phony on the screen. Understand?

MRS. COLLIER. *(unhappy)* I'll try to remember.

DICK. That's a good girl. I'm not going to rehearse this. I'm going straight away for a take, because very often the first attempt, even though it may be full of blemishes, proves to be the most naturalistic we get all day. *(DICK retires from the "set" to peer down the camera for a long moment at the final set up.)* Very well, gentlemen. The moment of consummation is come upon us. *(DICK steps away from the eyepiece of the camera to stand by its side. ALEX takes his place.)*

DICK. OK. OK, Alex?

ALEX. OK!

DICK. Roll for a number!

ALEX. Camera rolling. *(ALEX comes out and holds the clapperboard up to the camera.)*

JOE. Sound running!

JOE. Speed!

ALEX. Folliclean. Scene One. Take One. *(He claps the board and returns behind the camera.)*

DICK. Action!

PHILIP. Good afternoon, Mrs. Collier.

MRS. COLLIER. Good afternoon.

PHILIP. Now as you know I've come along here to talk to you about Folliclean, the miracle medicated shampoo.

MRS. COLLIER. Oh, yes.

PHILIP. Mrs. Collier it is true to say, is it not, that you are a regular user of Folliclean?

MRS. COLLIER. Yes, I am a regular fuser of ... I mean user of Folliclean.

PHILIP. Let's try that again. Mrs. Collier, is it true to say that you are a regular user of Folliclean?

MRS. COLLIER. *(parrot fashion)* Yes. I am a regular user of Folliclean.

PHILIP. And that your family are the same?

MRS. COLLIER. My family ... ? *(in a panic)* I haven't got a family...

PHILIP. I beg your pardon. Surely you have...

MRS. COLLIER. I mean they're not here. No one's here...

PHILIP. We know that but...

DICK. Cut it. *(The camera is switched off. DICK walks over to MRS. COLLIER.)* Now Mrs. Collier, I want you to relax. Just listen carefully to the questions and you'll be alright. You don't have to say anything you don't want to say, and we don't mind if you fluff a few lines. In fact it makes it more natural if you do.

MRS. COLLIER. I'm sorry, I'm that nervous...

DICK. Perfectly understandable. Just take your time. Shall we have another go?

MRS. COLLIER. Alright. *(DICK crosses back to stand by the camera.)*

DICK. Roll for a number. *(ALEX rubs out the number one and writes two on the take side of his clapperboard then holds it up to camera.)*

ALEX. Camera rolling.

JOE. Sound running!

JOE. Speed! *(ALEX comes out and holds the clapperboard up to the camera.)* Folliclean. Scene One. Take Two. *(He claps the board, and returns behind the camera.)*

DICK. Action!

PHILIP. Good afternoon, Mrs. Collier.

MRS. COLLIER. Good afternoon.

PHILIP. Now as you know, I've come along here to talk to you about Folliclean, the miracle medicated shampoo.

MRS. COLLIER. Yes.

PHILIP. Mrs. Collier it is true to say, is it not, that you are a regular user of Folliclean?

MRS. COLLIER. Yes I am a regular user of Folliclean.

PHILIP. And that your family are the same?

MRS. COLLIER. *(with an effort)* Oh definitely. I wouldn't buy them nothing else.

PHILIP. Can you tell us exactly what happens when you wash your hair with Folliclean?

MRS. COLLIER. Well it goes all foamy.

PHILIP. Into a thick lather, you mean?

MRS. COLLIER. Yes. A thick later.

PHILIP. And what did it do?

MRS. COLLIER. Do?

PHILIP. Yes. To your hair. What effect did it have on your hair? *(a nervous pause)*

MRS. COLLIER. *(vaguely)* What effect did it have on my hair ... I'm sorry I've gone and forgotten. *(She starts to giggle. PHILIP laughs, too, in a very strained way.)*

DICK. Cut it. *(The camera is switched off.)*

MRS. COLLIER. Oh, I am sorry.

DICK. Nothing to worry about, Mrs. C. Believe me you're in good company. The more you forget your lines, the bigger star you are.

MRS. COLLIER. Oh get away with you.

DICK. Perfectly true. I was directing an artist only the other day — a household name he was, too. Couldn't remember a word. Not even good morning. We'd either get good, or morning. Never the two together. *(MRS. COLLIER laughs.)* Mind you, of course, he hadn't been classically trained.

PHILIP. It was going very well, Mrs. Collier, believe me. Very well indeed.

MRS. COLLIER. *(more relaxed)* I suppose we have to start again from the beginning?

DICK. Not at all. We can pick it up from where we stopped. *(to PHILIP:)* I'll cover your question in a cut away.

PHILIP. OK. *(DICK goes back to camera. To MRS. COLLIER:)* The answer to my question about the effect of Folliclean on your hair is of course, that it got rid of your dandruff. Right?

MRS. COLLIER. Of course. I am a dunce.

DICK. Roll for a number.

ALEX. Camera rolling.

JOE. Sound running! *(MRS. COLLIER now seems perfectly relaxed as ALEX steps forward rubbing out the number two on the take side of his clapperboard, and substituting the number three. He holds it up to camera.)*

JOE. Speed!

TED. Folliclean, Scene one, Take three. *(He claps the board, and returns behind the camera.)*

DICK. Action!

PHILIP. And what effect did Folliclean have on your hair?

MRS. COLLIER. Well, it got rid of my dandruff.

PHILIP. It got rid of your dandruff, eh?

MRS. COLLIER. Yes. Cleaned it right out, it did.

PHILIP. Well, you can't say fairer than that, Mrs. Collier, can you?

Mrs. Collier. I suppose not.

Philip. Of course you can't. And tell me, did it ever return?

Mrs. Collier. No. I've never had another trace of it.

Philip. And does the same go for your family?

Mrs. Collier. They've 'ad no trouble neither.

Philip. That's marvellous. Mrs. Collier, can you tell us how it leaves your hair?

Mrs. Collier. Well, without the dandruff.

Philip. Quite so. But how does it look?

Mrs. Collier. Oh, it looks lovely. Clean and fresh-looking. You know. It smells nice, too, and I can always comb it alright.

Philip. In fact, Mrs. Collier, you would agree would you not, that it leaves your hair lustrous, shiny and manageable?

Mrs. Collier. That's right.

Philip. And do you find that Folliclean has had the same effect on the other members of your family?

Mrs. Collier. Yes, I'd say their hair was the same as mine. Shiny and clean and quite easy to manage.

Philip. Now, Mrs. Collier, do you think you could tell us how it was you came to use Folliclean in the first place? *(DICK motions for the camera to start tracking in. After a little delay it does so.)*

Mrs. Collier. Well, it's quite comical really. You see I was going to a funeral with my friend, Mrs. Barber, and as we was leaving the house she turned to me and said, "That blue's a bit light for a funeral, isn't it?" "Well," I says, "that's as maybe. But me beige is at the cleaners,

and I put a fag 'ole through the green." "Well what about
your black," she says, "What's wrong with that? Just the
thing for a funeral I'd have thought." She's always a bit
sarky, is Mrs. Barber, but there's no harm in it, not really.
Well I were that embarrassed, I can tell you. I mean to say
I couldn't hardly tell her about me dandruff now, could
I? But it wasn't 'arf bad — honest. Every time I moved,
down it came on me shoulders, thick and fast, like snow.
Of course black was out of the question. But *she* didn't
know that, did she? And she kept going on and on at me
though heaven knows she's not what you'd call such a
respectable person herself — not that I'm one for telling
tales out of school, mind. Well anyway, as I was saying,
she kept going on at me until I 'ad to tell her. Blimey she
didn't 'arf laugh! "You don't want to worry about a little
bit of dandruff," she says. "What you want is a good old
shampoo with Folliclean. That'll get rid of it in no time!"
"Straight up?" I says. "Straight up," she says. "I've been
using it for years and I haven't got a trace." "Well," I says
to myself, "what've you got to lose? Only yer 'air, and
that's hardly yer crowning glory at the moment, is it?" So
the next day I bought some — a little at first in a sachet,
and it worked a treat, so I've kept on with it ever since. It's
marvellous when you come to think of it. I mean for years
I couldn't wear black ... and now I don't hardly think
about it. And as for my hair — well, though I say it, as
what shouldn't, it's never looked lovlier. *(MRS. COLLIER
makes an expansive gesture and her wig slips forward over her
face. There is a moment of appalled silence.)*

DICK. Cut! Cut! *(The camera is switched off. Slowly MRS.
COLLIER takes her wig off, revealing the tangled mess of her own
hair beneath.)*

PHILIP. Whose bright idea was this, May I ask? ... Claire?

CLAIRE. Don't look at me, Phil. I knew absolutely nothing about it ... I swear it. We arranged for her to go to the hairdresser in the High Street this morning.

DICK. The Salon Pederast, wasn't it?

MRS. COLLIER. *(unhappily)* The Salon Pompadour ... I did go, but halfway home it came on to rain ... and well by the time I got here it was in a frightful mess ... and I didn't like to go back again.

PHILIP. I see.

MRS. COLLIER. So anyway I had this wig, which I didn't think was all that bad *(trailing off)* so I stuck it on.

PHILIP. Not firmly enough, unfortunately.

CLAIRE. It's a very good wig, Phil. It had me fooled.

MRS. COLLIER. It's not nylon or nothin' like that, you know. It's made of real 'uman 'air.

PHILIP. I suppose we can go with it if it's properly nailed down.

DICK. Why not? If we use shaving cream for ice cream, and ginger ale for lager, we should be able to use human hair for human hair.

PHILIP. Alright, alright. Claire, do you think you can fix it so it doesn't move?

CLAIRE. No problem.

PHILIP. Good. Then we'll go again as soon as you're ready. *(to MRS. COLLIER:)* Don't worry about the wig, Mrs. Collier. it was a most encouraging start. *(MRS. COLLIER darts a look at the clock.)*

MRS. COLLIER. Start?

PHILIP. Well, we haven't finished with you yet, you

know. We can't let our viewers know you're wearing a wig, or they might get the idea that Folliclean had made all your real hair fall out. *(He laughs his forced laugh. MRS. COLLIER smiles weakly.)*

MRS. COLLIER. Yes, I see. But you will hurry, won't you?

PHILIP. My dear Mrs. Collier, we could have been on our way out by now, if it hadn't been for that unfortunate accident.

MRS. COLLIER. *(distressed)* Oh dear ... I'm sorry ... It was stupid of me ... so stupid. *(DICK shoots PHILIP a venomous glance for his gaffe, then moves to comfort MRS. COLLIER.)*

DICK. Now don't worry, Mrs. Collier. You're doing fine. Yours is one of the best stories we've had in this series, and you looked marvellous as you told it — absolutely relaxed and natural. And what's more you didn't look at the camera once. It was quite remarkable.

MRS. COLLIER. Really?

DICK. Really. And what's more, we would have had to have done it once more anyway. We had a little technical trouble, I think, didn't we, Alex?

ALEX. I felt we were quite a bit late moving in, Dick.

DICK. Yes, so did I. *(to MRS. COLLIER:)* So there you are. You have nothing to blame yourself for. *(He smiles at her, and she half smiles back. CLAIRE moves in to fix the wig with some long pins, as DICK crosses to speak to BERNIE.)* Bernie, are you by any chance suffering from croup today?

BERNIE. No sir.

DICK. Or gout, or pellagra or any other debilitating

disease which prevents you from moving on my signal, and not half an hour later?

BERNIE. No, sir. Sorry, sir. Couldn't see it, sir.

DICK. Would it help if Miss Parker were to stand beside you, and at the critical moment bestow on you a dirty great sexy French kiss? Would that get you moving?

BERNIE. I don't think so, sir. I'm a married man, you see, and I don't get so much of the other anymore. What you're suggesting would more like do me up proper. *(JOE and ALEX laugh.)*

DICK. Well watch your step or I'll turn her loose on you. Now then, Claire, are we ready? Is Mrs. Collier's barnet as fixed and constant as the Northern star?

CLAIRE. Ready when you are, Dick. *(CLAIRE steps away from MRS. COLLIER. The wig is perfectly in position.)*

DICK. Right. First positions, everyone. *(BERNIE pulls the camera dolly back to its start mark.)* Are you ready, Mrs. Collier?

MRS. COLLIER. *(unenthusiastic)* I suppose so.

DICK. Is anything the matter?

MRS. COLLIER. Well, I've been sitting here for ever so long in the lights ... and me wig's hot ... and well you know, I'm a bit confused like.

DICK. Would you care to take a short break?

MRS. COLLIER. I don't want to hold you up, Mr. Richards ... but ... well, perhaps a short one.

DICK. Of course. Take all the time you need. Perhaps you'd like a little more tea or a glass of cold water, or something? *(MRS. COLLIER rather self-consciously leaves the "set" and goes to sit in an easy chair down stage right.)*

MRS. COLLIER. Water would be nice.

DICK. Claire? *(to ALEX:)* Save the lights. *(CLAIRE goes out to the kitchen to fetch the water.)* Let's do an atmosphere track while we're waiting. *(JOE wheels a boom mike into the center of the "set" and adjusts it. CLAIRE returns with a glass of water which she gives to MRS. COLLIER who drinks it gratefully. JOE returns to his place. DICK looks expectantly over to him.)*

DICK. *(to JOE: American voice)* Like now?

JOE. Anytime, sir.

DICK. Absolute quiet. Silence everybody. We're doing a buzz track. *(There is total silence on stage.)* Action.

JOE. Folliclean. Mrs. Collier. Room sound level effect tracks. Take one. I'm picking something up.

DICK. Cut it! ... Mrs. Collier, I thought you said you were alone here.

MRS. COLLIER. That's right.

DICK. Well, improbable though it may seem within the prosaic contours of a council house, we appear to have uncovered a ghost.

MRS. COLLIER. What do you mean?

DICK. I mean that something or someone appears to be doing an Albanian slide dance upstairs in one of the bedrooms. Listen. *(There is silence. We hear nothing.)*

MRS. COLLIER. I don't hear nothing.

DICK. Funny, I must have been mist ...

(We hear a dull THUMP. Then the FOOTSTEPS again.)

DICK. There they are again. You must have heard them.

MRS. COLLIER. *(very nervous)* It must be next door.

They're ever so noisy next door.

DICK. No. I'm afraid it's upstairs. Claire be a good girl, and take a look. *(CLAIRE nips up the stairs as MRS. COLLIER rises in consternation from her chair.)*

MRS. COLLIER. *(in panic)* No! Don't go up there!

(She moves to follow CLAIRE up the stairs, but stops at their foot. There is silence except for the sound of CLAIRE'S footsteps clattering along the corridor above.)

CLAIRE. *(calling down)* It's locked!

(We hear the sound of a KEY turning in a lock. A silence follows, then a short SCREAM. CLAIRE rushes down the stairs and into the room, looking wildly behind her. A longish silence is followd by shuffling, scratchy FOOTSTEPS moving slowly along the corridor, and then starting to descend the stairs. A clawed panther's paw comes into view through the bannisters, resting on the top stair that is visible. After a further pause the figure of a panther comes into sight, and slowly slinks on all fours down the stairs. The creature, now snarling, crawls into the room as the other instinctively back away from it. Suddenly it bounds upright and the skin falls off to reveal the pasty, overweight figure of MRS. COLLIER'S 14-year-old son, REGINALD. He is wearing a schoolboy uniform, which is rather too small for him.)

MRS. COLLIER. Reginald! *(REGINALD turns his head to take in the room, and his eyes flick quickly over the film men and their equipment, before coming to rest on the figure of his mother. As he addresses her, she takes a quick step backwards.)*

REGINALD. Hullo, mother. You see I've escaped. Have you been telling them how I killed father?

CURTAIN

ACT II

The time is a moment later. No one has moved.

REGINALD. Well then, have you?

MRS. COLLIER. You're quite disgraceful. Coming in 'ere talking like that!

REGINALD. Have you told them about Dad?

MRS. COLLIER. *(shouting)* Go back to your room immediately, REGINALD!

REGINALD. What? For you to lock me in again — just because you think I'm not safe. No fear.

MRS. COLLIER. *(hissing under her breath)* Just you wait till I get you alone.

REGINALD. *(coldly)* Idle threats, mum, idle threats. You know what I do to parents. *(He suddenly becomes aware of the film unit watching.)* Hullo! You never told me the people from the films was coming. *(to DICK:)* Hey mister! How did you like my performance? Pretty scary, eh? It's from my favorite film. "The Curse of the Cat." It's all about this giant panther which goes about carving people up. In the end it turns out it isn't a real panther at all. It's this chap what works at the local garage dressed up in a panther skin going prowling round at night waiting for a chance to get his claws in the crumpet. *(He growls.)* He's got a grudge against society, see?

MRS. COLLIER. Reginald. You go up to your room this minute, or I'll...

REGINALD. *(interrupting)* Yes? *(MRS. COLLIER remains silent. REGINALD points to the camera dolly.)* What's that?

DICK. It's a dolly. It moves the camera.

REGINALD. It's a pretty daft name, isn't it?

DICK. *(blandly)* No dafter than Reginald.

REGINALD. *(a sudden flash of anger)* 'Ere, you watch it. You don't know *all* my names. They're John Reginald Halliday.

MRS. COLLIER. Reginald really...

REGINALD. I'm named after Christie of Rillington Place. He was a right one, he was, killing them birds and then 'aving them. And I tell you, mister, you wouldn't take the mickey out of *me,* if you knew what *I'd* done. *(He points to the "flags" on the lamps.)* What are them things?

DICK. *(pointing to the "flags")* These things?

REGINALD. Yeah.

DICK. They're called flags. They help mask off the lamps to make them more directional. The lamps, as you have probably noticed, are all of different sizes. That is a 5K. That is a 2K. That is a pup. That is an inky, and that is a basher. Those are the tracks on which the dolly runs, and that is the camera mounted on the dolly. It is a blimped Mitchell with variable speed motor. We are shooting on Eastman stock at an exposure of fl1, and we would very much like to get on. So would you mind having it away as nimbly as possible on the tips of your blunt little toes?

REGINALD. A basher and a dolly, eh? Sounds kinky.

DICK. To the pure all things are pure, Reginald. When you're ready Mrs. C. *(MRS. COLLIER comes forward uncertainly, and takes up her position in the "set".)*

MRS. COLLIER. Reginald, if you're going to stay, sit down and be quiet.

REGINALD. You don't believe me do you? You want convincing. Shall I tell you *how* I killed my father?

DICK. *(indulgently)* Not just now, if you don't mind. Why don't you have a chat to our sound gentleman over there. He's been trying to murder his old woman for years. You might give him a few tips. *(DICK moves over to arrange PHILIP and MRS. COLLIER in their chairs.)*

JOE. It's quite true, you know, Sonny. I've tried arsenic in the coffee, and cyanide in the shrimps. I even tried dropping an electric heater in her bath once.

REGINALD. *(interested in spite of himself)* What happened?

JOE. I forgot to turn it on. *(JOE laughs. REGINALD looks daggers at him.)*

DICK. Absolute quiet please! First positions! Lights! Now, Mrs. Collier, we'll start straight away, this time with Philip asking you how you came to use Folliclean, and you telling us your story. OK?

MRS. COLLIER. What? Where I talk about me black?

DICK. Exactly. *(to Grips:)* Which means Bernie, you start moving in as soon as Mr. Charles has asked his first question. And not one jot nor tittle later. Roger?

BERNIE. Right, guv.

DICK. Are you ready, Philip?

PHILIP. All set.

DICK. Right. Stand by! *(pause)* Turn over...

ALEX. Camera rolling. *(ALEX comes out and holds the clapperboard up to the camera, and returns behind the camera.)*

JOE. Sound running!

ALEX. Camera rolling.

JOE. Speed!

DICK. Bags of enthusiasm this time, Mrs. Collier.

TED. Folliclean. Scene One. Take Four. *(He claps the board.)*

DICK. Right! And action!

PHILIP. Tell me, Mrs. Collier. How did you first come to use Folliclean? *(The camera starts to track in slowly.)*

MRS. COLLIER. *(uneasy and nervous)* Well I was with my friend Mrs. Barber and we was off to a funeral. All of a sudden as we was going down the street she turns to me and says "That blue's a bit light for a funeral, isn't it?" "Well," I says, "that's as maybe, but me beige is off at the cleaners, and I ..."

REGINALD. Whose funeral was it?

DICK. *(furious)* Cut! Cut! Cut! Bloody cut! *(The camera is turned off.)* Would you mind! We're shooting sound here! It's difficult enough, without your interruptions.

REGINALD. Why don't you *ask* her whose funeral it was?

DICK. I really don't see that it matters.

REGINALD. Oh but it does. You see, it was dad's.

DICK. *(wearily)* Are you going to start all that nonsense again?

REGINALD. Nonsense! You're going to wish it was. *(Laughs.)* Buy Folliclean! Murderers' mothers use it!

PHILIP. Mrs. Collier. I must appeal to you. This is obviously some family joke you have between you, but I'm afraid we're all finding it a bit embarrassing. Perhaps you could persuade Reginald to leave us for half an hour. We won't be longer.

MRS. COLLIER. Reginald! Go up to your room at once.

These gentlemen don't want to hear your silly made-up stories.

REGINALD. Go up to my room?

MRS. COLLIER. Right now! You heard. I shan't ask you again.

REGINALD. *(with menace)* Quite right. You shan't ask me again. And you shan't lock me up again to prevent me telling about what I did to dad.

MRS. COLLIER. You're a wicked fibber. *(helplessly to PHILIP:)* He's got some really nasty habits, Mr. Charles. Talking about his dad like that.

PHILIP. *(uncomfortable)* Yes. I can see he has.

MRS. COLLIER. Sometimes I just can't do nothing with him.

PHILIP. *(authoritative)* Reginald, you heard your mother. Would you please go back to your room?

REGINALD. My father was a bastard; a soapy-haired bastard. He had to go. It's very difficult 'cos your dad's bigger than what you are — much bigger, so you can't get at him. Unless of course he's lying down — as he was on the beach at Tenby. He had his eyes closed and the sockets was white compared to the rest of his face. I aimed for the Adam's Apple, and chopped it through with my tin spade. The blood came pouring out with little bubbles on it like on a pint of beer, and ran down over my sand castle and into the moat I'd dug around it. I was bloody scared, but I thought it's the last time you say *(parody precise middle-aged man's voice)* "No, I don't think we can possibly allow that," or "Do I have to remind you yet once again, Reggie, who's the governor," or hold me by the back of the neck with your soapy hands. *(A pause. The atmosphere of disbelief has changed.)*

MRS. COLLIER. Oh, you're disgusting. Disgusting, do you hear?

REGINALD. What a hypocrite you are mum. It was you what finished him off.

MRS. COLLIER. I won't listen to no more of this. I simply won't. A joke's a joke, but this has gone far too far. You will apologize to the gentlemen at once and go straight to your room.

(The front door BANGS.)

MRS. COLLIER. *(in alarm)* It's Christine, home from school. She'll be wanting her tea I expect.

(CHRISTINE, the daughter of the house, comes through the door, and carefully closes it behind her. She is a rather pretty, solemn girl of 13, short for her age, and neatly dressed in school uniform. She carries school books and a satchel which she puts down on a chair in the center of the room. She looks about her, examining the startled faces of the film crew who have been shocked into immobility, with great interest.)

CHRISTINE. Hullo, everybody! *(Pause. They stare at her.)* Well don't all speak at once. *(Giggles.)* You all look as if you've been turned to stone. Like Lot's wife.

MRS. COLLIER. *(vaguely)* Who, dear?

CHRISTINE. Lot's wife, mum! We're doing it at school. It's funny to think of a woman being a voyeur of sodomy, isn't it?

DICK. Why? Like most women she wasn't bent. Just plain nosey.

CHRISTINE. Who are you?

DICK. Dick Richards.

CLAIRE. I'm Claire Parker. You're Christine, aren't you?

CHRISTINE. Quite correct.

CLAIRE. I don't know whether your mother told you, but we're making a television advertisement here today. *(pointing them out)* That's Philip, Alex, Joe & Bernie.

CHRISTINE. How do you do?

PHILIP, ALEX, JOE, BERNIE. Hi. Hello there. Good afternoon, etc. *(A general buzz to relieve the tension.)*

CHRISTINE. Can I be in it?

DICK. Your mother doesn't think it's a good idea.

CHRISTINE. She wouldn't. All mothers are jealous of their daughters. They can't help it.

MRS. COLLIER. Christine!

REGINALD. What about fathers?

CHRISTINE. What about them?

REGINALD. I was talking about dad before you came in.

CHRISTINE. *(surprised)* You didn't tell them?

REGINALD. Yes I did. I was annoyed with mum for locking me in my room.

CHRISTINE. *(mock admonitory)* Was that wise?

REGINALD. *(defiant)* I don't care. I'm not ashamed of it. I'm glad I killed him. *(CHRISTINE draws herself up.)*

CHRISTINE. *(haughtily)* I beg your pardon, Reginald. I've told you a million times, *I* killed him.

REGINALD. *(heated)* Don't be bloody daft. What? A girl like you?

MRS. COLLIER. *(desperate)* Do be quiet, both of you.

Christine, I'm sure you've got a lot of homework to do ...
Reginald, go back to your...

CHRISTINE. *(Ignoring her. She talks to DICK and PHILIP.)*
My dad was a silly man, mister. We called him Dr. No.
Everything was no with him. — No you can't 'ave no
elecution lessons; no you can't 'ave no lessons in deport-
ment; no you can't learn nothing about fashion modelling. He called it *(parody father's voice)* "Knowing your
place, my girl." Well mister, I knew where my place was
going to be, alright, when I grew up. Modelling on the
French Riveria. Wearing them fancy sun glasses, and
them swim suits with the holes in 'em. Having dinner
with some depraved French count. Well, you can't do
nothing like that if you haven't been learnt how to model
can yer?

PHILIP. No, I suppose not.

DICK. It's the first time I've heard that the aim of
education is din dins with a kinky count.

CLAIRE. I can see it must have been frightfully frustrat-
ing for you.

REGINALD. Christine's the frustrated kind. Dreams all
day long of the high life on the Continong. You know she
told me once her ambition was to live with a master
cracksman. They was going to sunbathe all day on their
private yacht, and steal jewels and pictures all night, from
the villas on the Coty D'Azurey.

CHRISTINE. Why don't you keep your cakeole shut, you
pissy little runt, you.

REGINALD. Don't mind her. She forgets she's a lady
sometimes. Now me — I'm always the gent — you know,
like Steed. A gent, and a man of action, mind you. I'm all

suave and silky and talking posh, when suddenly me spotless white cuffs shoot out, and me dukes get moving so fast they're like a blur — you can't 'ardly see them. *(He acts it out.)* One in the 'ooter, one in the breadbasket, a couple more to the mush, a quick chop to the froat, and it's all over, Like I said, I'm a gent, but I'm a killer when roused.

CHRISTINE. *(derisive)* Killer! You couldn't kill time.

REGINALD. I killed dad!

MRS. COLLIER. *(screaming)* Stop it! Stop it!

CHRISTINE. You perishing little liar. *(desperately, to the others:)* I did it. I found him asleep on the beach. I went back to the picnic basket to get the long pickle knife. Then I crept up on him through the sand dunes, slowly, slowly on my stummick so he wouldn't hear. Then I stuck it right through his eye so he got pinned to the sand like a butterfly. Of course he twisted about something 'orrid, but I belted him with a big flat stone on the head, and that quietened him. You should have seen the blood. It was coming up like a fountain through his eye. *(to REGINALD in disdain:)* Then you came up and hit him with your spade. You wouldn't have dared hit him when he was alive.

REGINALD. *(angry)* You're barmy. You hardly hit him at all with that silly knife. If I hadn't cut his throat with that spade — he'd still be here. *(pleading)* Don't you remember how the blood poured down over the sand castles and filled up the moat?

CHRISTINE. Yes. That was smashing! But it came from what I done.

REGINALD. Ooh! You bloody liar. Don't you remember...

MRS. COLLIER. *(shrieking)* Reginald! Christine! *(slowly they turn to face her)*

CHRISTINE. *(softly)* Are you shocked, mum? You shouldn't be.

REGINALD. After all, it was you what finished him off. I mean finally.

CHRISTINE. Yeah! You made sure, didn't you, mum? In the cave.

REGINALD. That's it. In the cave. When you was all alone.

MRS. COLLIER. *(as if in a trance — half playing a game)* Oh no! That's not right! I just hid him. *(A pause. A stir goes through the unit.)*

CHRISTINE. What for?

MRS. COLLIER. Well, I couldn't just leave him there on the beach.

REGINALD. Very considerate, mum.

CHRISTINE. Well, after all, she was married to him.

REGINALD. I suppose so.

CHRISTINE. Oh, yes, she was. For better or for worse. She had to make him comfy.

REGINALD. But not drown him.

CHRISTINE. Well it wasn't so much drowning, as putting him out of his misery.

REGINALD. Whose side are you one, anyway?

CHRISTINE. *(prim)* I'm just being h'objective.

MRS. COLLIER. I didn't drown him. He were already dead. When I got him in that cave. I only 'id 'im in there to protect you two.

REGINALD. And that's the case for the defence, my lord. *(The two children giggle together.)*

CHRISTINE. We know different. We were naughty, disobedient children.

REGINALD. Yeah. You see mum we didn't go back to the hotel like you told us. We stayed and watched.

CHRISTINE. From a ledge above the cave. Dad came alive. He was moving about.

REGINALD. And you held his head under water.

MRS. COLLIER. *(wildly)* I was trying to revive him.

CHRISTINE. *(mock dramatic)* Slowly his struggles got weaker ... and weaker ... a shuddering sigh escaped him ... and then he lay still.

REGINALD. *(mock sad)* There was a star fish floating in the water by his head.

CHRISTINE. Poor old dad!

REGINALD. Poor old dad! *(They giggle together. After a while it dies away into a long silence. The CREW members look at each other in horror, then BERNIE, PHILIP, DICK, ALEX & JOE huddle together for a whispered conversation, downstage.)*

BERNIE. *(sotto voce)* What the hell's going on here? Are they all mad, or what?

DICK. *(sotto voce)* Don't ask me. It wasn't my research department who selected them as an ideal television family.

PHILIP. *(sotto voce)* What are we going to do? We just can't carry on as if nothing had happened.

ALEX. *(sotto voce)* I suppose we'll have to send for the police.

PHILIP. *(sotto voce)* Dear God. I suppose there's no chance that the whole thing's a gag?

ALEX. *(sotto voce)* A gag?

PHILIP. *(sotto voce)* You know — to send us up.

ALEX. *(sotto voce)* I suppose it could be, they're pretty blatant about it all, aren't they? I mean if they'd really done it, they'd keep mum.

DICK. *(sotto voce)* Even if they'd disposed of dad you mean ... Why should we resent a little fantasy in the suburbs? We should cherish it. Perhaps we could even try and work a little of it into the shot. You know have the kids dressed up as leopard men or Thuggee silk cord stranglers or something ... I suppose you're right. It would come as a nice surprise to Mr. Oldwife.

PHILIP. *(sotto voce)* He mustn't find out about any of this. *(The GROUP breaks up. PHILIP approaches MRS. COLLIER.)* Look here, Mrs. Collier, you realize how serious all this looks to us.

MRS. COLLIER. *(as if awakening from a trance or ceasing to play a game)* Serious?

PHILIP. Of course. If it's all true, we shall have to report it to the police.

MRS. COLLIER. The police?

PHILIP. Naturally. You must see there's nothing else we can do...

MRS. COLLIER. *(desperately)* The police? But surely you're not taking all this seriously? *(She laughs wildly.)* It's only a game the children play.

PHILIP. And you too?

MRS. COLLIER. Er ... I join in sometimes.

PHILIP. It all sounded pretty convincing to me. *(The chilren crowd around PHILIP pleading in a half-jocular, half-scared manner.)*

REGINALD. Don't go to the police, mister. Don't.

CHRISTINE. It's like mum says. It's only a game. Honest!

REGINALD. We was only having you on, mister.

CHRISTINE. We often play it. Passes the time.

PHILIP. Well, it's a fairly macabre game but I suppose that's none of my business. Look, if you promise to behave yourselves, and let us finish this commercial in peace, we'll say no more about it. OK? *(The children nod their heads in dumb acceptance.)*

DICK. Just as a matter of casual interest, Mrs. Collier, where is their father? *(She stares at him, then looks away.)* Mrs. Collier? *(a further silence)*

MRS. COLLIER. He's.........

(The DOORBELL chimes loudly. Everyone freezes. Finally CLAIRE PARKER goes and opens it. LIONEL YOUNGHUS-BAND, the manufacture of Folliclean, stands on the threshold. He is a tall, sandy-haired Northerner of about 45, still trim and good looking. He is a shrewd and highly successful businessman, who treasurers a reputation for eccentricity, and a certain obscure sense of humor the butt of which is usually the decadent Southerner. PHILIP turns to face him and immediately drops into the obsequious attitude common between advertising agents and their clients. His face, however, clearly betrays that they couldn't have come at a worse time. CLAIRE goes outside, closing the door behind him.)

PHILIP. *(shakily)* Mr. Younghusband! ... Er ... how very nice of you to pay us a visit. *(LIONEL advances into the room, looking about him as he does so.)*

LIONEL. *(Lancashire accent)* Aye. Well, I just popped in to see all's going well. As you know it's not my policy to interfere with, or spy on, my advertising agency in any way. Afternoon all.

PHILIP. Can I introduce you, sir. This is Mrs. Collier, our star. *(LIONEL looks at MRS. COLLIER appreciatively.)*

LIONEL. 'Ow do!

PHILIP. *(very much doing his best under the circumstances)* Mrs. Collier, this is Mr. Younghusband, our client. He makes Folliclean.

MRS. COLLIER. *(still shocked)* Pleased to meet you. *(They shake hands.)*

LIONEL. *(looking around him)* Well, you keep a decent place, Mrs. Collier ... Nawt fancy, but wholesome.

MRS. COLLIER. Thank you.

PHILIP. And these are the children — Reginald and Christine.

LIONEL. 'Ow do kids ... Alright then?

REGINALD. As well as can be expected.

CHRISTINE. Under the circumstances, that is.

LIONEL. Circumstances? What circumstances?

PHILIP. *(quickly)* They're obviously very excited about the filming, sir. It doesn't happen every day.

LIONEL. No, I don't suppose it does.

REGINALD. It's dead monotonous round 'ere, and no mistake. Nothing hardly ever happens 'cept bingo and bowling, and fish and chips, and a punch-up Saturday nights.

CHRISTINE. And an occasional murder.

REGINALD. Silly of me to forget that.

CHRISTINE. It's the long night of the soul, alright, if you live in Plaistow, mister.

PHILIP. *(desperately)* Now now, kids. Let's not get carried away. Every district has the same thing. *(to MR.*

YOUNGHUSBAND:) I'm sorry, sir. They're very high-spirited.

LIONEL. I can see they are. *(to MRS. COLLIER:)* They must be quite a handful.

MRS. COLLIER. Yes, they are.

LIONEL. They're about the same age as my pair. And carry on much the same way. You know — imaginative.

MRS. COLLIER. *(shudders)* Yes.

PHILIP. *(desperate)* Mrs. Collier, why don't you take the children off, and give them their tea while I explain what we are doing here, to Mr. Younghusband? I'm sure they must be hungry.

MRS. COLLIER. Yes, I suppose they are. Come on you two. *(She moves towards the kitchen.)*

REGINALD. Can we have baked beans on toast?

MRS. COLLIER. Alright.

CHRISTINE. And eggs?

MRS. COLLIER. Baked beans will be quite enough, Christine.

CHRISTINE. *(mutinous)* And boiled eggs, mum.

REGINALD. Two eggs each. *(MRS. COLLIER looks at the company for a moment and decides to capitulate gracefully. She smiles thinly.)*

MRS. COLLIER. Very well. Come alone, and quick about it.

REGINALD. We'll be back.

CHRISTINE. You bet. I flip for father figures. *(The children follow their mother into the kitchen. PHILIP propels DICK forward, hurriedly to cover the gap.)*

PHILIP. Do you know Dick Richards, our director, Mr.

Younghusband? I'm sure you've met before.

LIONEL. Aye ... He had the same shirt on. Very fetching.

DICK. It's been washed since.

PHILIP. *(hurriedly)* We've got a very strong story in this house, sir. The lady couldn't wear dark clothes until a neighbor told her about Folliclean.

LIONEL. Is that so?

PHILIP. Yes sir. Over the years she'd tried other cures of course, but they didn't help her. Naturally we're bringing that point out very strongly.

LIONEL. I should damn well hope so. You want to get plenty of family stuff in too. You know the sort of thing — Mrs. Collier couldn't go out with her husband in the evenings because she was too embarrassed. All her lovely frocks were covered in telltale scurf. When suddenly along came Folliclean, and bingo! All her problems vanished. Mr. Collier's proud to be seen out with his wife now!

PHILIP. *(embarrassed)* Well, of course there is a slight difficulty about...

LIONEL. Don't worry, lad. I'm not telling you how to make the picture. There's no point in keeping a dog and barking yourself. That's what I say.

PHILIP. Quite so, sir.

LIONEL. All I'm saying is something very simple. I've said it before and I'll say it again. People are interested in other people. It's only natural, isn't it?

PHILIP. Oh, of course, sir.

LIONEL. Exactly. It's no use flying in the face of human nature. And I do mean face; because every face tells its own story — and that's what people want to see — each other. All I'm saying, is this, lad. If you are lucky enough to find a well-set-up family like this one — use it. I mean to say — this is an ideal family. Attractive mother, handsome lad, smashing little lass — nowt wrong wi' it. Honesty, hard work and family feeling — they radiate from this place. You can feel it as you come in the door. Perhaps it could use a dog or a pussy to complete the picture, but I suppose you can't have everything in this life. *(suddenly struck by a thought)* 'Ere. Where's dad? *(a pause)*

PHILIP, DICK. *(together)* He's away. He's dead.

LIONEL. *(confused)* What?

DICK. Mrs. Collier's husband is dead, sir. An unfortunate bathing accident, I believe. *(LIONEL is suddenly aware of Mrs. Collier behind him. the children appear silently in the kitchen doorway.)*

LIONEL. Oh! I am sorry. You must forgive me for being tactless. I didn't see you standing there.

MRS. COLLIER. I just came back while the water was boiling. It's quite all right. Really.

LIONEL. I can't apologize enough — going on that way.

REGINALD. Think no more of it. It's a natural mistake. Anyone could have made it.

CHRISTINE. Yes, anyone. After all, most families have fathers, don't they?

LIONEL. Aye, lass, they do. And as I say, I'm sorry.

CHRISTINE. I feel so sorry for mum you know, mister. It must be so lonely, not having a man about the place. Not that she ever complains, mind.

REGINALD. What about me, then?

CHRISTINE. You're not a man. You're a boy.

REGINALD. Well, I've done a man's work.

CHRISTINE. Oh, don't start all that again. You couldn't do your shoe laces up by yourself.

REGINALD. Don't be stupid. I've done up more than shoe laces and you know it.

CHRISTINE. I know nothing of the sort. I know you're the most barefaced...

MRS. COLLIER. *(strained)* Children, please stop that bickering. What will Mr. Younghusband think of you?

LIONEL. Don't fret yourself on my account, Mrs. Collier. I get plenty of all that at home. *(He smiles reassuringly at her. She responds weakly and walks back towards the kitchen.)*

MRS. COLLIER. If you'll excuse me. I expect the water's boiling now. *(She goes through into the kitchen, taking the children, who have not moved from the doorway, firmly with her.)*

LIONEL. *(to PHILIP:)* I hope there's no reference to how Mr. Collier came to pass on in that commercial, Mr. Charles.

PHILIP. Er ... oh none. None whatsoever, sir...

LIONEL. Good.

PHILIP. Perhaps, sir, you would like Mr. Richards to explain briefly to you, what he is doing in the film.

LIONEL. Aye. If he can spare the time. *(DICK produces the falsest of false smiles.)*

DICK. It would be a pleasure, Mr. Ol ... Younghusband. Kill the lights. *(He leads LIONEL to a small table stage right and they sit down, where they are joined by PHILIP. Their heads come together in earnest discussion. BERNIE, JOE and ALEX sit together down stage, holding a desultory sotto voce conversation in whispers.)*

JOE. I wish someone would explain to me what the hell we're doing in this house.

BERNIE. We're waiting our turn to be carved up by the kids. Didn't you know?

JOE. Not me, mate. I'm not hanging around to be chopped up by them two. *(He shakes his head in disbelief.)* Cor, what a turn up, eh? Would you believe it?

BERNIE. *(with bravado)* Personally man, I don't. But then I'm not shit-scared like you. I think they're just having us on.

JOE. Don't give me that. They did him in alright. I'm for having the law sort it out. What do you say, Alex? *(ALEX scratches his ear judicously.)*

ALEX. I'd leave it to the gov to sort out, mate. He'll know what to do.

JOE. Well, I'm not going to turn my back on them kids, I can tell you. *(The conversation continues in undertones we don't hear, then dies away altogether as the group splits up.)*

DICK. Well in my view, this whole subject must be treated with the greatest discretion. The school as it were of Lytotes rather than Hyperbole.

LIONEL. You what?

DICK. Understatement rather than overstatement.

LIONEL. Why didn't you say so in the first place?

DICK. I was just about to qualify my remark with an explanation.

LIONEL. Oh you were, were you? Well, I don't like the idea of understatement any road. This is an advertising film, not a ruddy poem—

DICK. To this end we use a documentary technique — rather flat naturalistic lighting, the subject's own home, rather than a studio and no attempt is made to induce her to speak copy.

LIONEL. I suppose it would be too much to expect that Mrs. Collier does a little selling.

DICK. But for the most part the professional interviewer will be doing the hard sell.

LIONEL. It's my opinion that most Southern professional interviewers are so nambly-pamby they couldn't sell a dildo to a castaway nymphomaniac.

DICK. *(barely keeping his temper)* There's little I can do, if you're unhappy about the interviewer, Mr. Younghusband. Mr. Charles, I believe, was approved by you yourself...

LIONEL. Come on lad, now don't get shirty. I'm only having my bit of fun. It's not Philip Charles I'm unhappy about if you must know, it's the whole story that Mrs. Collier's telling. *(PHILIP CHARLES, hearing his name mentioned, hastily rises from the dolly and crosses to stand beside MR. YOUNGHUSBAND.)* All this talk of graveyards and funerals ... You must admit it's pretty depressing. You'd be much better off introducing the kids and letting them tell the story of having no father, but what a smashing mother they've got, and then bring out that though she's a widow woman living on a limited income, she nonetheless spends a high proportion of it keeping them clean. In my opinion that would be most effective.

PHILIP. With respect, sir, I don't think we'd get away with that. As you've seen yourself, the children are far too

... er, excitable to tell a coherent story in the time we've got.

(The children poke their heads round the kitchen door, their mouths half full of food.)

LIONEL. Oh, I'm sure you'll be able to manage them alright, Mr. Charles. After all you're a "professional interviewer," aren't you?

PHILIP. The children aren't the only difficulty, sir. You see Mrs. Collier doesn't want...

LIONEL. Mr. Charles, I want the children to tell the moving story of how their widowed mother does her best for them. Understood?

PHILIP. Of course I take your point of view, sir, but with respect, we feel that the funeral story is one of the strongest and most memorable we've had, and that therefore...

LIONEL. Mr. Charles, you are not taking my "point of view" if I may say so. You're not taking it at all. I don't want my product associated with a boneyard, and I'm not going to have it. I've told you what I want, and if you're not prepared to give it me, there are plenty of other advertising agencies in this town, who I'm sure, will. Do I make myself perfectly clear?

PHILIP. Yes sir.

LIONEL. So let's get the kids out here, and get on, shall we?

(The children suddenly rush out of the kitchen, pursued by MRS. COLLIER.)

MRS. COLLIER. I'm sorry. They insisted on seeing what was going on.

REGINALD. And why not? You can't always keep us locked away, mother.

CHRISTINE. *(to MRS. COLLIER, designing to be overheard by LIONEL:)* Yes. Even if you won't let us be in the film, at least we can still watch.

LIONEL. Won't let you be in the film? Why not?

MRS. COLLIER. *(confused)* I ... I didn't think it was right.

LIONEL. Not right? Come now. Everyone likes to see kids in't films.

MRS. COLLIER. Well, I'm sorry. I weren't told nothing about no kids when I was first asked by Miss Parker.

LIONEL. *(sternly)* Mr. Charles, did you know about this?

PHILIP. *(stuttering)* Er yes, Mr. Younghusband. We didn't consider the children vitally important to Mrs. Collier's funeral story.

LIONEL. And why not, Mr. Charles, particularly as you are well acquainted with me views on family-feeling?

PHILIP. I'm sorry, Mr. Younghusband. It must have been an oversight. I know Mrs. Collier was asked as soon as Miss Parker got here today and I asked her myself later but she refused both times. Of course we were all most disappointed.

REGINALD. *(to PHILIP:)* Never mind, mister. We can still make it up to you. We'll do our best, honest we will.

CHRISTINE. A real human drama — full of passion and hate; life and death. The searing story of a desperate fight for freedom against overwhelming odds and the right to pursue happiness.

LIONEL. What are you on about, lass?

CHRISTINE. David and Goliath, mister. The little one destroying the giant.

REGINALD. The underdog striking back. The worm turning.

CHRISTINE. The right to live free, breathing God's clean air.

REGINALD. The right not be pushed around.

CHRISTINE. Man is born free but is everywhere in chains.

REGINALD. Lavatories of the world, unite. You have nothing to lose but your chains. *(The laugh together.)*

LIONEL. *(to MRS. COLLIER:)* They're a bit of a comedy team, your two, and no mistake.

PHILIP. I'm afraid it's those lively imaginations of theirs again, sir. They can't stop showing off.

LIONEL. Well it's up to you to stop them, isn't it?

REGINALD. *(piteously)* Forgive us our lively imaginations, mister. You see we've had to compensate for not having a dad.

CHRISTINE. We've had to learn to tell each other stories and keep Mum cheerful.

LIONEL. *(to PHILIP:)* That's exactly what I was saying. They know they've got a smashing mum. *(to CHRISTINE:)* She looks after you alright, your mum, doesn't she? *(The two children cling theatrically to MRS. COLLIER'S skirts.)*

CHRISTINE. She's the best mum in the whole wide world.

REGINALD. She don't have a lot of money, but she always turns us out decent.

LIONEL. Listen, would you kids behave yourselves if I was able to persuade your mother to let you be in the film?

CHRISTINE. Behave ourselves? What do you mean?

LIONEL. I mean cut out this larking about and simply tell the story of what it's like to have no dad, and how clean and well turned out your mother has always kept you since ... well, since you've been by yourselves.

REGINALD. What, be film stars? Just give us the chance, mister, we'll show you.

CHRISTINE. Yes, we'll show you. Like so many young kids today, all we need is the break.

LIONEL. Well, Mrs. Collier, what do you say to that?

MRS. COLLIER. No, Mr. Younghusband, I don't think they should...

LIONEL. Come now, as a favor to me.

MRS. COLLIER. I'm sorry. I've got enough trouble with them, without their getting swollen heads. *(Both children give her a withering look.)*

REGINALD. *(slowly and deliberately)* I wonder what Mr. Younghusband would say if I told him that with only a tin spade...

CHRISTINE. *(equally slowly)* and of course not forgetting a certain rather long pickle knife we...

PHILIP. Now don't start getting excited again. *(urgently)* Surely, Mrs. Collier, you must see it would be better if you allowed them to make an appearance. Better for everybody.

MRS. COLLIER. *(wearily)* Oh, alright. *(The children cheer. to children:)* But you must do exactly what Mr. Charles and Mr. Richards tell you. Is that clear?

CHRISTINE. *(trying to look voluptuous)* Of course. As long as it's savage, sexy and sophisticated.

REGINALD. And I can be cool, charming and utterly callous. You know the sort of thing I mean — women find me irresistible, men fear my fierce anger.

DICK. There should be no problem. Christine can play Alain Delon, and you, Reginald, can be Bette Davis.

REGINALD. Very funny!

PHILIP. *(hastily)* Why don't you both go and finish your tea, and we'll call you when we've worked out the new set up and story line. *(REGINALD is inclined to be mutinous but CHRISTINE takes his arm and steers him into the kitchen.)*

CHRISTINE. Come along, Reginald. We need to prepare ourselves. *(They make a grand Exit.)*

LIONEL. Right, well we've got that settled at last. Now remember, Mr. Richard, I won't abide any of that showing off in't film, so mind you keep a firm hand on 'em. If they've got to do something, let's see them doing normal, homely things — you know, like playing with a Meccano set or mending a bike or someat.

DICK. I was thinking maybe that we might have a scene where Mrs. Collier is preparing to take them out to the seaside for the day. Reginald could perhaps be playing with a bucket and spade, while Christine could be packing a picnic basket.

LIONEL. Well I'm not sure that ... bathing is quite the thing...

PHILIP. *(hastily)* Perhaps you could spare Mr. Richards

and myself for a few moments, sir. We are going to have to replot the whole commercial.

LIONEL. Go right ahead, Mr. Charles. As I say I don't keep a dog and bark myself. I'll have a sit down and a little chat with Mrs. Collier here. *(PHILIP gives DICK a furious glance as he drags him off to the "set.")*

PHILIP. *(sotto voce)* What are you trying to do — wreck everything?

DICK. I was merely trying for a new wrinkle in the Player-King routine.

PHILIP. *(hard)* Leave it alone, Dick, and let's both try and survive. *(They go into a huddle round the camera and we see them plotting the new commercial, in mumbles and dumbshow throughout MR. YOUNGHUSBAND'S scene with MRS. COLLIER. The crew are also involved in a huddle down stage left and from time to time glance in MR. YOUNGHUSBAND'S direction, and we hear the word "police" from JOE, and "later" from ALEX. LIONEL, meanwhile, has gone and sat down by MRS. COLLIER stage right.)*

LIONEL. You don't mind if I sit with you, do you?

MRS. COLLIER. Course not.

LIONEL. You're a very handsome woman, Mrs. Collier, and no mistake. It's an honor to have you in one of my films.

MRS. COLLIER. *(nervous)* Oh! Well, thank you very much. You seem to be the only one here who knows what he wants.

LIONEL. Well you've got to be firm. Is something the matter, Mrs. Collier?

MRS. COLLIER. The matter?

LIONEL. Aye. You don't seem at ease. No one has

seemed at ease since I've been here, come to that.

MRS. COLLIER. I expect it's all the excitement. We've never had nothing like this before.

LIONEL. I thought it might have been me who'd upset you — you know when I talked about your husband and all.

MRS. COLLIER. Oh no. That was alright.

LIONEL. I mean it can't be easy with struggling along without a husband with them kids of yours. They're even dafter than my two. Do they go on like that all the time?

MRS. COLLIER. *(weary)* A lot of it.

LIONEL. Well, I've heard of some kids' games in my time but they beat the lot. What were all that about David and Goliath and lavatory chains and tin spades and pickle knives?

MRS. COLLIER. *(Shudders and shakes her head. Whispers.)* I've no idea.

LIONEL. *(oblivious)* I think they must be up the pole. Mind you, I'll say one thing for them. They certainly had a great affection for their father. They both obviously miss him like hell. *(MRS. COLLIER nods dumbly. LIONEL still hasn't noticed her distress.)* When was it he died exactly?

MRS. COLLIER. *(flustered)* Er — about fourteen months ago.

LIONEL. Aye. Time enough for them to have got a bit out of hand. There's no substitute for a man about the place. Or a woman either, if it comes to that. They recognize it themselves. I'm sure you're doing your very best to remedy the deficiency.

MRS. COLLIER. *(Smiles wanly at him.)* I do what I can.

LIONEL. Tell me, Mrs. Collier, how exactly did he come to drown?

MRS. COLLIER. *(Shudders violently)* Please don't let's talk about it.

LIONEL. *(seeing her distress)* No, of course not. It was tactless of me. That bathing's a tricky thing though. What with the currents and the jelly fish and all.

MRS. COLLIER. I'm afraid I'm not much of a swimmer. Never fancied it somehow — even as a girl. I liked games though — lacrosse and netball and running. I was good at running. I could run for hours — always out in front. It's funny really. My mum used to come and watch me at the school sports. "What do you want to run so quick for?" she used to say. "You'll never catch a man that way!" *(Laughs.)*

LIONEL. She knew right enough, your mum did. *(pause)* Mind you, I don't expect a woman like you would have to try that hard.

MRS. COLLIER. Oh, I don't know, a woman on her own with two kids.

LIONEL. Well I'm in the same boat, lass — since my wife died.

MRS. COLLIER. I'm sorry — I didn't know.

LIONEL. It's a few years back now.

MRS. COLLIER. Well there you are. I suppose it can't be much fun being a man left alone with kids.

LIONEL. *(Gives her a grateful look.)* No. I sometimes reproach myself for being too soft with them while she was alive. They put on her a lot, you know. Marjorie's always saying they put her in her grave, but that's just so much hogwash. Tricks and mischief don't do for you, leastways not as much as leukemia.

MRS. COLLIER. That's what she had, was it, leukemia?

LIONEL. Aye. *(reflectively)* She were a big woman, with a grand smile on her, though it was strange, you know. It didn't go up like most people's. It just went straight across. I used to tell her it were there to keep her cheeks apart. She got very thin very sudden. The doctors could do nowt for her. Her veins leaked, you see.

MRS. COLLIER. How dreadful. You must have been really cut up seeing her go that way.

LIONEL. Aye. But I don't like to think of her as she was then. I like to remember when she was younger. You know she had a great feeling for food. She'd handle a rhubarb tart as gently as she would a baby. *(Laughs.)* And look at it in much the say way.

MRS. COLLIER. *(musing)* It's funny how women are with children. When they're little, they're so lovely and cuddly and then all of a sudden they're not any more. I don't know where they get their ideas from half the time.

LIONEL. Well, basically, they're good kids. They may lack a little fatherly discipline at the moment, but that's only natural.

MRS. COLLIER. Oh, yes, they're fine, I suppose. You must have the same problem.

LIONEL. With no woman around, you mean? Yes, I suppose it makes a difference. A man can't do it all. They need the balance: the man to say "no" and the woman for them to get round to say "yes."

MRS. COLLIER. Oh, come on, I don't think you're like

that for a moment. I bet your two twist you round their fingers every day.

LIONEL. Don't you believe it. *(Intimate smiles! DICK and PHILIP break up their meeting and move toward MR. YOUNGHUSBAND.)*

PHILIP. I think we've got it all straight now, sir. Would you like Mr. Richards to run over it with you, or perhaps show you how it will be through the camera.

LIONEL. No, no. It would only be a lot of double talk, I expect.

PHILIP. I'm sure Mr. Richards would explain in simple language.

LIONEL. You know my son Sydney is learning photography at school — they've got a proper film society and all there — and he told me that most of the technical terms are just so much hogwash to bamboozle the man in the street, and that it's all pretty simple, really.

DICK. Next time you come, you must bring him along with his little Polaroid Swinger, he might be able to give us a few tips on how to use it.

LIONEL. Are you being impertinent, Mr. Richards?

DICK. No, just flippant. You must forgive my rather bad keep-the-client-happy manner. I'd make a lousy account executive.

LIONEL. Just so long as you don't make a lousy film director. *(to MRS. COLLIER:)* I must be off now. It's been a real treat meeting you. Just grand. *(They shake hands, warmly.)*

MRS. COLLIER. It's been very nice meeting you too. Goodbye, Mr. Younghusband. *(LIONEL moves towards the door.)*

LIONEL. Don't say goodbye, lass, just say "Olive Oil."
Afternoon all. *(A murmur of "Goodbye, sir.")* Goodbye, Mr.
Charles. I'm looking forward to seeing an affecting story
about this poor widowed lady — One with real heart.

PHILIP. We'll do our best, sir. It's been good to have
you with us. Let me see you to your car. *(PHILIP shakes
shakes MR. YOUNGHUSBAND'S hand and shepherds him out
of the door. There is a long silence. Everyone stands about not
knowing quite what to do. ALEX appraoches DICK.)*

ALEX. The boys are worried about the kids, Dick. Joe's
all for going to the police. I expect some of the others are
too. *(DICK ponders for a moment, and then suddenly aware that
all eyes are on him, as the director, comes to a sudden
decision.)*

DICK. *(shouting to the unit)* Gentlemen, as you are all
only too well aware, we were in the middle of a trifling
domestic drama here, when our agency's client so unfor-
tuitously arrived. I would like to prevail on you to re-
strain yourselves for a fifteen minute tea break to allow
Mr. Charles and myself to resolve matters with Mrs.
Collier. *(There is a murmur among the crew. MRS. COLLIER
starts guiltily and goes out to the kitchen, ostensibly to see after the
children, but equally obviously to stave off the meeting with DICK
and PHILIP.)*

DICK. In other words — brew up and belt up! *(A light
laugh relieves the tension. ALEX stoops to pull the cable connection
to the generator and the film lamps go out. ALEX, JOE and BER-
NIE file out of the door talking softly among themselves.)*

(CLAIRE pokes her head round the door.)

CLAIRE. The cup that cheers? *(DICK, now left alone on stage, nods silently. She comes into the room carrying two cups and some sandwiches on a tray, which she puts down on the table stage right. DICK produces a flask of brandy from his pocket and pours some into his tea. He offers the flask to CLAIRE but she shakes her head and sits down.)*

DICK. Let it on this occasion inebriate. *(He takes a long pull at the tea.)* Christ! What an afternoon! *(They look at each other. He nods with sad comprehension. She kisses him suddenly, very quickly.)*

CLAIRE. *(brightly)* Tell me what happened. I fully expected us to have lost the account by now, and to find the house infested with meaty men in blue.

DICK. *(Northern accent)* Lionel never flushed out our guilty secret.

CLAIRE. And it *is* out guilty secret, isn't it?

DICK. Meaning?

CLAIRE. Well, you don't really think the kids were playing a game do you?

DICK. Yer pays yer money and yer takes yer choice.

CLAIRE. Come on Dick — you saw how evasive Mrs. Collier was when you asked her where their father was.

DICK. Maybe she'd forgotten. It's not unknown for women to mislay their husbands.

CLAIRE. *(patiently)* Hiding your head won't make it go away, you know.

DICK. I suppose not.

CLAIRE. Well, do you think they did it?

DICK. Oh don't be so bloody relentless, Claire. What do you want me to say — that those pestiferous children

did for their doubtless even more pestiferous daddy? ...
Well of course they did. It's obvious, isn't it?

CLAIRE. I think so. and Mrs. C?

DICK. I don't know. She probably had to finish him off
to protect them.

CLAIRE. You've got to tell the police.

DICK. Oh I agree, but not immediately. I mean let's do
the commercial first, then tell the police after it's been on
the air a few times. It'll create a sensation when the story
breaks. Instead of the normal television commercial
family, sunk, as usual, in irredeemable archness, we will
be presenting a whole homicidal gang. "The Killing
Colliers," and have all three of them, dressed up in
trench coats and soft velour hats, holding tommy guns ...
And what's more Philip could do the commentary ...
(commentator voice) With the help of their mother, these
children wiped out their father, but they couldn't wipe
out dandruff, until one day she gave them Folliclean, the
medicated shampoo that murders scurf.

CLAIRE. For God's sake, Dick, do stop fantasizing
everything.

DICK. Alright. For your sake I'll go to the police.

CLAIRE. Don't do it for my sake, sweetie. Do it for your
own sake.

DICK. Why don't we get Philip to do it?

CLAIRE. You know he won't. He's got his precious
account to protect.

DICK. That's a fine reason, I must say.

CLAIRE. It's better than yours.

DICK. You mean you prefer the coward to the
dreamer. So much for the romantic illusion.

(PHILIP comes in through the front door, banging it behind him.)

PHILIP. *(angry)* Look here, Dick, why did you have to go and offend Lionel?

DICK. I'm sorry, I couldn't help it.

PHILIP. Couldn't help it! You know how important that account is to my agency.

DICK. Yes, and you'd do anything to keep it — even become an accessory after the fact of murder, wouldn't you?

PHILIP. That's more than we know. We were just getting it all straight when Mr. Younghusband arrived.

DICK. You know they did it alright, but now of course, thanks to your grovelling pusillanimity it's too late to do anything about it. Lionel's obviously taken a fancy to Mrs. Collier — and he's determined to have his gallant widow commercial, otherwise he'll move the acount. On the other hand if you make it, and the story comes out, as it's bound to do in time, with those babbling children, sounding off all over the place, he'll still take the account away, and also sue Wren and Whiltshire for swingling great damages into the bargain. I can just hear him talking to your managing director. *(parody LIONEL'S voice)* Don't try and tell me that Mr. Charles didn't know they'd got together and killed their dad. Of course he did. And to think that he went ahead and filmed those murdering kiddies talking about my produce! He's made me a laughing stock, that's what he's done — a bloody laughing stock! A pal of mine called me the other day and he said "Lionel! I saw that commercial of yours and it's a dead giveaway. Their scalps may be clean, but you can tell they're maniacs by the shapes of their skulls."

PHILIP. For Christ's sake will you shut up. *(a pause)*

CLAIRE. What are you going to do, Phil? *(PHILIP contemplates for a moment in silence.)*

PHILIP. We'll go ahead with the widow commercial, as we discussed it before. If it doesn't work, I will at least have something to show Mr. Younghusband, to prove to him that we tried to do what he wanted, but that the kids were uncontrollable. He knows all about the difficulties of filming children. He's not a fool.

CLAIRE. And you'll risk possible future exposure?

PHILIP. It's a reasonable bet. After all, he can't actually prove that we knew anything, can he, in spite of Dick's hilarious prognostications?

CLAIRE. What about the crew? ... What about me? Are we all supposed to keep quiet, too?

PHILIP. I'm sure you'll be loyal, Claire.

CLAIRE. It's hardly a question of loyalty, is it? As DICK says, if we keep quiet we'll become accessories.

PHILIP. *(shouting)* What do you want me to do?

CLAIRE. Ask Mrs. Collier again.

PHILIP. That won't get us anywhere. If they did it, she's not going to admit it to us now, is she?

CLAIRE. I don't know ... Dick?

DICK. I suppose Philip's right ... My advice is to let sleeping husbands lie. *(CLAIRE slowly gets up and moves towards the door.)*

PHILIP. I'm glad you recognize what side your bread is buttered on at last.

DICK. It's not the same as yours, believe me.

PHILIP. Get the boys back, Claire, will you. We'll set their minds at rest for them. *(CLAIRE shoots a pitying look at DICK and goes out of the door.)*

PHILIP. Right, let's get on with it. I think I'll leave Mrs. Collier for a while, and start with the kids. *(calling)* Reginald! Christine!

(The two children come into the room with a promptness which suggests that they have been listening to the whole of the previous conversation. They look angelic. They have put thier best clothes on, and their hair has been neatly brushed. Their expressions are demure.)

REGINALD. Did you call?

PHILIP. Yes. We're ready for you now.

CHRISTINE. How do you think we look?

PHILIP. Super. I wouldn't have recognized you.

CHRISTINE. Good grooming is essential to a film star, wouldn't you say?

PHILIP. As is good behavior on the set. For example, we don't want any more references to killing your father. Do you understand?

REGINALD. Not a word.

CHRISTINE. We'll be as silent as the grave.

PHILIP. I want Mr. Richards to tell the camera crew that he died a natural death.

REGINALD. That would be the most prudent way.

CHRISTINE. It would set everyone's mind at rest.

PHILIP. Good. All I shall want from you is a brief account of what it's been like living without a father, and how hard your mother has tried to keep you both clean and neat on a limited income, OK?

REGINALD. Orphans of the storm?

CHRISTINE. Little Nell?

PHILIP. Just use your own words. Now we'll go over to the set and Mr. Richards will arrange us as he wants to.

(ALEX, JOE and BERNIE Enter as the children and PHILIP move over to DICK RICHARDS. He seats PHILIP in the chair occupied previously by MRS. COLLIER and REGINALD and CHRISTINE either side of it. He then turns to greet the crew.)

DICK. Welcome back, gentlemen. I am most relieved to be able to tell you, that we have ascertained that the information you received earlier from these children concerning the death of their father, was in the nature of a hoax, and that he in fact died naturally.

ALEX. Thank God for that. *(The crew mutter amongst themselves as they go to their positions.)*

BERNIE. Well, I'm glad it came out alright for you, sir… If I was their mother, I'd give them both a damn good hiding, talking about their old man like that.

JOE. She's the worst, egged them on she did. You heard her. Personally, I've still got me doubts.

BERNIE. Go on. She probably doesn't know which way she's going with them two kids…

DICK. Quiet now, everyone please. *(The chatter subsides as DICK moves over to ALEX.)* As we're running a bit late, Alex, I thought we'd keep the same set up for the kids as we had for Mrs. Collier. You can adjust OK for the hair can't you?

ALEX. No problem. Just give me a second.

(LIGHTS up. ALEX starts to rearrange his lights somewhat with the help of the electrician so that they spotlight the children's hair and faces, but shade the rest of them.)

DICK. *(to ALEX:)* Put a 35 on Alex.

ALEX. 35 it is, govnor. *(ALEX changes the lens and DICK takes his seat on the camera dolly. When ALEX has finished, he looks through the camera at the set up.)*

DICK. *(to BERNIE:)* Slowly in, Bernie. *(BERNIE pushes the camera down the rails towards the set up. About halfway in, DICK stops him.)* Hold it there. *(DICK continues to look through the camera. (to BERNIE:)* Ease out a fraction. *(BERNIE pulls the camera back a few inches.)* That's it. Perfect. Peg it there. *(He gets off the dolly as BERNIE chalks his position on the side of the rail. At the same moment, ALEX withdraws from the set, and goes to sit on the camera dolly.)*

ALEX. It's all yours. Dick.

DICK. Right. First positions, please. You ready, Philip?

PHILIP. Ready and waiting.

DICK. Then let us immortalize it. Roll for a number!

JOE. Sound running!

ALEX. Camera rolling.

(ALEX comes and holds the clapboard up to the camera.)

JOE. Speed!

DICK. Call this version B, and mark the board with a B. *(ALEX scribbles a B on the board, and holds it up to the camera.)*

ALEX. Folliclean. Version B. Scene one, Take one. *(He*

claps the board and withdraws.)

PHILIP. My name is Philip Charles. These delightful children are Reginald and Christine. Some time ago their mother, Mrs. Florence Collier, was unhappily widowed. Nonetheless, in spite of the sudden economic privations, Mrs. Collier has always insisted that her children's health and cleanliness should not in any way be sacrificed. *(addressing the children rather than the camera)* Children, could you tell our viewers, briefly, what it's meant to you to grow up without a father?

REGINALD. We've missed him, of course, sir. You're not like other children.

CHRISTINE. *(soulfully)* There's no gruff voice behind the morning newspaper.

REGINALD. No heavy footsteps coming up the path each night.

CHRISTINE. No rough tweed jacket smelling of tobacco to cuddle up against before bedtime...

REGINALD. No one to take you to the football, or help fly your kites on the common.

CHRISTINE. No one to carve the joint on Sundays...

REGINALD. No one to sail your boat with on the pond. No one to say "well done, son" when you've scored a goal.

PHILIP. *(desperately)* I'm sure we all sympathize with your misfortune, children, but surely your mother has done everything she could do to fill his place.

CHRISTINE. She's a different shape for one thing.

(The children giggle together. Suddenly they fall silent as the front door BANGS. Into the room strides BILL COLLIER, a dapper,

middle-aged, ex-sergeant major. He surveys the disarrayed room coldly. The children shrink away from him fearfully. His accent when he speaks is refined parade ground.)

DICK. Cut it! Save them! *(The camera is switched off.)*

BILL. What the hell is going on here?

PHILIP. My name is Philip Charles. I'm a TV producer. Might I ask who you are?

BILL. Me? I'm Bill Collier.

DICK. *(in astonishment)* What? Mrs. Collier's husband?

BILL. That's right. Here, what's the matter, man? You look as if you'd seen a ghost.

CURTAIN

ACT III

The time is a moment later. No one has moved.

DICK. I think Mr. Charles is just the teeniest bit bur-
prised to see you, Mr. Collier. And come to that, so am
I.

BILL. Oh you are, are you? Well the feeling's mutual, I
can tell you.

PHILIP. *(recovering)* I am sorry. It was quite a shock. How
do you do? *(He extends a hand which is ignored.)*

BILL. That's all very well, but what are you doing here,
I'd like to know. Let's 'ave your name and number.

PHILIP. I'm Philip Charles of Wren and Wiltshire — the
Advertising Agency. This is Dick Richards our director...

BILL. That doesn't give you the right to come barging
into a man's home with all that paraphernalia.

PHILIP. We've got permission, Mr. Collier. My assistant
Miss Claire Parker explained it all to your wife.

BILL. Well she didn't say nothing to me. Not a little dickie bird. I might say I take a very dim view of things being
done behind my back. A very dim view h'indeed. In fact I
can really get quite mean and vicious with people who
deceive me. *(to the children:)* What are you kids up to?

REGINALD. Nothing. We ain't doing nothing.

CHRISTINE. We was just talking to the man.

BILL. What are you two hiding?

REGINALD. Nothing. Honest.

85

BILL. I 'ope not. I will not 'ave deceit in this 'ouse. Is that understood?

REGINALD. Yes. *(CHRISTINE nods her head.)*

BILL. Better get in the kitchen then for the moment. I'll deal with this. *(The two children slink into the kitchen.)*

PHILIP. I'm sure there's been no intention of deceiving you, Mr. Collier. If I can just explain how all this happened, and what we're doing here.

BILL. You've got sixty seconds, and that's your lot. Starting now! *(PHILIP goes over to the camera dolly, and takes from a box on it a large stop watch — more a time-keeper's clock — set in a wooden case. It is large enough to be seen clearly at a distance of at least 20 yards. He turns it to face the audience and starts it.)*

PHILIP. We represent a product called Folliclean, a medicated shampoo designed to combat dandruff. As you may have seen, we have been running a series of commercials on television in which housewives explain how they and their families came to Folliclean, and what it has done for them. They usually introduce some semi-humorous tale of family life into their narrative to make it more interesting, and it is on the basis of these incidents, coupled of course with the strength of their cure stories that we select the housewives. We employed an agency to do some preliminary house to house research, and they sent us a short list of likely names and addresses. We sifted through the list and your wife was one of the eight subjects we decided to film, because she had an unusually good story to tell about her discovery and successful use of Folliclean. We asked her if she would agree to make the commercial, and she said yes and so here we are. And that explanation, incidentally Mr. Collier, took precisely one minute flat. *(PHILIP stops the clock. The hand how an exact minute has passed since it started.)*

BILL. What all that in a minute? You're having me on.

PHILIP. See for yourself. *(He shows BILL COLLIER the clock face.)* It's amazing what you can do in a minute.

DICK. Minute steak. Minute men. Minute Waltz.

BILL. *(puzzled with DICK)* What's he on about? *(A thought strikes him.)* 'ere. How did you know it would be a minute without looking?

PHILIP. We get used to measuring time in the TV commercial business, Mr. Collier.

BILL. I hope you're paying people for taking it up.

PHILIP. One hundred pounds and a year's supply of Follicelan.

BILL. *(Calls.)* Florence! You wouldn't like to make it two hundred quid and keep the Folliclean would you?

PHILIP. No, I'm afraid I can't quite see Mr. Younghusband, the Managing Director of Folliclean, agreeing to that.

(MRS. COLLIER comes into the room. She starts back violently when she sees her husband, and then looks guiltily at PHILIP and DICK.)

MRS. COLLIER. Hello, Bill.

BILL. Hello, Florie. You seem surprised to see me. You might call it put out. Struck all of an 'eap. Paralyzed with indecision.

MRS. COLLIER. It's just that I didn't expect you.

BILL. *(hard)* I'll bet you didn't. That's why you fixed up this little caper. A hundred nicker your hard working old man would never have know damn all about.

MRS. COLLIER. I wasn't trying to do nothing behind your back, Bill. Honest! It was going to be a surprise when you saw us all on the telly.

BILL. *(malicious)* Surprise, eh? Well I planned me own rotten surprise. *(to PHILIP:)* They thought I was in Yorkshire this week. But I swapped it with me Kent week. I knew this skyving lot was up to something.

PHILIP. You do a lot of travelling then, Mr. Collier.

BILL. I'm on the road. Kent one week. Yorkshire the next. All over the country. Leather goods is my line. Belts, bridles, straps. It's surprising what a great number of things 'as got to be restrained in this world.

PHILIP. Yes, I suppose so. I've never really thought of it.

BILL. Well, you think of it. 'Orses, boys, loonies. My guvnor makes the straps for straight-jackets. There's a thing for you. I mean you wouldn't think of a thing like that would you? Not normally, that is. But someone's got to do it.

PHILIP. I imagine so.

BILL. Dead right they 'ave. You couldn't 'ave nutters running wild all over the loony bin making out they was Napoleon, now could you? I mean, if I couldn't put you in a straight-jacket you couldn't tuck your hand in the front of your jacket for a start, could you? *(PHILIP shakes his head, bewildered. The whole business of producing a television commercial with the Collier family, is getting too much for him.*

DICK illustrates his next remarks by holding his right breast with his left hand.)

DICK. Well, I'd feel a right tit, if I did.

BILL. Eh? Now come off it. Don't take the mickey. It's a serious job making them straps. Scientific. My guvnor goes and has pukka meetings with the trick-cyclists before he makes 'em. I mean you don't want them going hurting themselves, do you? *(Laughs.)*

DICK. What sort of man is your guvnor?

BILL. I was his sergeant-major. We've always seen eye to eye, you might say. In the stinking jungle together, we was. We didn't 'arf have a few laughs, out there I can tell you. Of course we had a few sticky moments with the top brass now and again; — they didn't like some of his methods. But there it is. You can't expect to get away with it all the time can you? Wait, I'll show you. 'Ere, Florie, get the beer out and give the gentlemen a drink. I shan't be a tick. *(MR. COLLIER goes upstairs to the bedroom. MRS. COLLIER goes to the kitchen. DICK and PHILIP move downstage.)*

DICK. I must say he looks pretty good for a man who's been in the sea since last year.

PHILIP. He certainly does. What a bloody good job we didn't go to the police.

DICK. Dishonesty is always the best policy.

PHILIP. Dishonesty? What do you mean? I never really believed they'd actually done it. *(PHILIP glares at DICK who smiles back insouciantly.)*

DICK. For my part I rather wish the kids *had* done it and saved me the experience of meeting him. If ever I saw a walking candidate for a spade through the glottis, or a knife through the cornea I see it now. I must say, I'm profoundly disappointed with those children. No spirit of get up and go. No real enterprise. Just talk, talk, talk!

PHILIP. Well, why do you think they lied like that?

DICK. It's obvious. They hate his guts. Aunty wish-fulfilment strikes again.

PHILIP. And Mrs. Collier? She went along with it because like the kids she *also* wanted to believe it was true.

DICK. *(sarcastic)* Bravo! What kept you?

(PHILIP makes a warning gesture of silence as MRS. COLLIER returns with the beer on a tray. She looks guiltily at them.)

MRS. COLLIER. *(defensively)* What are you looking at me for? I told you it was only a game.

PHILIP. I was wondering what exactly we were going to do with you now.

MRS. COLLIER. *(looking fearfully up the stairs)* Now? Surely you don't want to do no more?

PHILIP. Well, Mr. Younghusband *is* expecting some sort of commercial for his money today, Mrs. Collier. We know he doesn't like the graveyard story, and *(glancing up the stairs and lowering his voice)* under current circumstances we can hardly use the gallant widow approach, can we?

MRS. COLLIER. I suppose not. No. *(DICK smiles triumphantly at PHILIP, who looks angrily away.)*

MRS. COLLIER. *(sotto voce)* I told you it was a game, but you went and told him it was true. I had to keep up the fib didn't I?

PHILIP. *(sotto voce)* I'm sorry Mrs. Collier, you got us all a little confused. The point is, what to do now.

DICK. I wouldn't have thought that it was that difficult. All you have to do is to reward dull Lionel with dull Lionel's dull idea. Group the kids round Mrs. Collier's feet and have her describe how she keeps their hair clean while they are doing *(parody Lionel's voice)* normal homely things like playing with a Meccano set or mending a bike or someat.

PHILIP. *(sotto voce)* How do we explain to him the absence of the widow angle?

DICK. *(sotto voce)* Simply tell him that Mrs. C got upset every time there was a reference to her dead husband. *(A man as strong on (Northern voice)* "family feeling" *(normal voice)* as he is, should respect that.

PHILIP. *(doubtfully)* I suppose so.

MRS. COLLIER. I had to let him go on thinking he was dead ... but of course, really I was that embarrassed...

(BILL COLLIER comes down the stairs with an album of loose photographs. MRS. COLLIER looks at him nervously.)

MRS. COLLIER. Alright. But you'll have to ask my husband.

PHILIP. Leave that to me.

BILL. Got that beer poured out yet, Florie?

MRS. COLLIER. I could only find Pale Ale I'm afraid. I don't think it's too bad.

(BILL Enters the room.)

BILL. There's no such thing as bad beer, my dear. You ought to know that by now. *(MRS. COLLIER hurries over to the tray of beer and starts to pour if out. BILL notices the photograph album still in his hands.)* Here, have a shufti at this lot. *(DICK takes the photographs and riffles through them under BILL COLLIER'S instruction.)* That's me in Beirut with Lofty Langhorn and Freddie Chambers. He got a bit cheeky later on and we had to sort him out. This one here's near K.L. — Kuala Lumpur to you, that's the guvernor and me at the Christmas '60 party; and 'ere we are again in K.L. What a lark, eh?

DICK. My God! What are you up to here?

BILL. *(Laughs compacently.)* That there was the guvnor's idea. He wanted to be carried abaht like flipping Cleopatra on her litter. Took the wheels off a rickshaw. Them four's Gook prisoners, and that's me at the back. *(DICK peers at the photograph closely.)*

DICK. What's that you're carrying?

BILL. That was me bullock goad. Got it from a lad on the rice fields. Kept them fellers moving along at a crack-ing pace, I can tell you. If there's one thing I can't stand it's a malingering Gook. *(Pause. He pours more beer.)* Life's not the same as it was and that's a fact. You've got to work for your beer money these days. There's precious little left after the wife and kids 'ave 'ad their whack! Not that I'm complaining, mind. There's nothing in this 'ere world like 'aving a loving wife, and two fine upstanding kids as what can't wait for you to return to them of an evening. It's a beautiful feeling gentlemen. It makes a man proud. *(MRS. COLLIER smiles wanly at him. There is an uneasy silence.)*

PHILIP. Perhaps we ought to get back to work. We've still got a little bit to finish off with your wife and the children. That's, of course, if you don't mind, Mr. Collier.

BILL. You carry on. Don't you take no notice of me.

PHILIP. Thank you, Mr. Collier.

DICK. Quiet everyone. Quiet please. *(to JOE:)* Let's hear the last one, back, please.

(JOE runs the tape back so it emits a high garbled NOISE as it does so. He stops it suddenly and switches it to play.)

REGINALD'S VOICE. *(from the tape recorder)* Hullo, mother! You see I've escaped. Have you been telling them how I killed father? *(BILL COLLIER drops his beer glass. JOE turns it off.)*

BILL. *(hoarsely)* 'ere. What's been going on? That was Reggie's voice.

MRS. COLLIER. *(wildly)* A joke ... A game.

BILL. *(furious)* " 'Ave you been telling them 'ow I killed father?" A joke? I'll give you bloody joke. *(He whirls around to look for REGINALD.)* Where's that boy?

(He marches into the kitchen and drags the cowering REGINALD into the living room by the ear. CHRISTINE follows them, apprehensively.)

BILL. You there. What do you mean by this?

REGINALD. I ... I ... I ...

DICK. It was a game of pretense I invented, Mr. Collier, in order to get the children in the mood to act.

BILL. Oh. So it was you was it? Well what sort of a game is that, eh? Telling them they killed their father.

DICK. We weren't actually referring to you, Mr. Collier, but to a character in a story I told them and asked them to act out. You may remember Reginald says "Hullo, Mother. You see I've escaped." Well this was from a Nazi prison I asked them to imagine they were in.

REGINALD. *(eagerly fabricating)* Well I escaped see by cutting the guard's throat who brought me grub. I stole his keys and crept out past the guards. When I got home I found this huge Nazi Ober-lieutenant threatening Mum and Christine. He was going to rape them.

CHRISTINE. He was telling us, how, if we wanted to be good Nazis we should betray our father, but we refused. Reggie overheard this conversation, and pretended to Mum he'd already killed his father in order to protect him.

REGINALD. Yeah. I'd hidden me dad in the barn yer see, under the hay where they'd never find him.

CHRISTINE. It was a smashing game. *(There is a pause. MR. COLLIER looks about the room, and sees that everyone is looking at him. Embarrassed, he suddenly explodes into laughter.)*

BILL. The things you kids get up to! Nazi prisons! Hiding people in barns. You kids will be the death of me! *(He suddenly realizes what he has said and stops laughing abruptly.) The kids and he stand locked in enmity. Suddenly he turns to DICK.)* All the same I think this playacting is bad for them. Unsettling. I didn't give no permission for this lark and as the man of the 'ouse I should 'ave been consulted.

So, if you don't mind you'd best pack up your gear and get off out of it.

PHILIP. Mr. Collier. My firm has invested a great deal of time and money in this commercial. I must ask you to reconsider. We'll only be a little time now.

BILL. I'm sorry, Mr. Charles. Deceitful carrying on is something I can't abide — and there's far too much of it going on 'round here for my liking. You've got five minutes, starting now!

PHILIP. I've just had an idea, Mr. Collier, which you might care to consider. I was wondering if, after we've finished with your wife, whether you would consent to star in a commercial all by yourself.

BILL. Are you trying to get 'round me?

PHILIP. Not at all, Mr. Collier. Our client who was here a little while ago expressed particular disappointment that you were taking no part in the filming. I know he would be delighted if you consented to appear.

BILL. *(flattered)* I'm not at all sure I'm all that cut out for theatricals. I don't hold with 'em.

PHILIP. This isn't theatricals, Mr. Collier. You would be simply recounting a real life incident that happened to you in connection with how you or your family came to use Folliclean.

BILL. Well of course — put that way...

PHILIP. I'm sure there was one, wasn't there?

BILL. Was what?

PHILIP. An incident which was connected with your discovery of Folliclean.

BILL. Oh, definitely. But I don't know whether it would be worth anything to you.

PHILIP. It's certainly worth another hundred pounds to you.

BILL. Another hundred nicker?

PHILIP. Making two hundred pounds altogether.

BILL. You did say all by myself?

PHILIP. Of course. *(A pause. BILL COLLIER considers how to about-turn with dignity.)*

BILL. I dunno! Perhaps I've been too 'asty. I mean ter say, you 'aving spent all that money and that.

PHILIP. Good. Then it's settled.

BILL. You can use the kids in the picture too if you want, but I won't have then rabbiting.

PHILIP. Anything you say, Mr. Collier. Perhaps you'd be so kind as submit to a little make-up, now, while we finish with your wife.

BILL. *(half eager, half derisive)* What? Powder and rouge stuff?

PHILIP. Not rouge, Mr. Collier, just powder. If you don't have it you look at death's door under the lights. Claire! Where's Claire?

BERNIE. She's outside in the car, sir.

PHILIP. Well let's have her in then. *(BERNIE goes to the front door opens it and calls out.)*

BERNIE. Miss Parker, please!

BILL. I don't want no beauty spots neither.

PHILIP. Don't worry, Mr. Collier. When you see yourself on television no one will realize you're made up.

(CLAIRE PARKER follows BERNIE into the room.)

CLAIRE. You wanted me?

PHILIP. Yes. Would you make up Mr. Collier, please?
(CLAIRE is shaken.)

CLAIRE. Mr. Collier? Is he...?

PHILIP. *(hastily)* Yes. He is.

CLAIRE. ... I thought he was ... you mean the kids were just...

PHILIP. Exactly.

CLAIRE. Then he isn't...

PHILIP. *(urgently under his breath)* No. I'll explain later. Just shut up and get on with making him up.

CLAIRE. It's difficult enough to believe in the Resurrection, but this is ridiculous.

PHILIP. Mr. Collier, this is my assistant, Miss Claire Parker. She will be making you up.

BILL. Pleased to meet yer.

CLAIRE. Pleased to meet *you. (She stares hard at him. He flinches.)*

BILL. Is something the matter then?

CLAIRE. Nothing, Mr. Collier. Nothing whatsoever. It's just that I like to study the bone structure of my victims.

BILL. I see.

CLAIRE. It must give you so much satisfaction to be the center of an admiring family, Mr. Collier. You must tell me about them. I'm sure they get up to all sorts of lively tricks...

(She leads MR. COLLIER through to the kitchen to be made up. PHILIP comes downstage to join DICK.)

DICK. It's a pure waste of film shooting him. You can't

let Lionel Midwife know Mrs. C's got a husband after all.

PHILIP. I know that, and I've got no intention of showing it to him, but he'd have thrown us out of the house otherwise. By the way I did admire your Nazi prison story. It really saved our bacon.

DICK. Don't mensh. As a matter of fact I can't wait to hear *his* story. I'll bet it's all set in some...

PHILIP. No more fantasies, Dick, if you please. Let's just dispose of Mrs. Collier while we've got the chance. *(to Mrs. Collier:)* Mrs. Collier, we're just about ready for you. Do you think you could find those things for the children to play with?

(MRS. COLLIER gets into a whispered huddle with the children. After a second, REGINALD and CHRISTINE run up the stairs to their bedrooms. DICK moves into the set to confer with ALEX.)

DICK. *(to ALEX:)* The kids will be on the floor here at Mrs. Collier's feet. Mrs. Collier is going to introduce them, and as she mentions their names we'll ease back and tilt to frame them. OK?

ALEX. You realize of course that both their heads will be predominantly top lit.

DICK. That'll be alright. It'll give them the angelic halos they both so richly deserve, and at the same time conceal most of Reginald's acne.

ALEX. I'll need them to stand in.

(REGINALD and CHRISTINE come down the stairs and Enter

the room. The former carries a large model sports car, and the latter a book of fashion plates.)

DICK. Very good, those props will do admirably. Now if you would just sit on the floor, you Reginald here, and you Christine there, we'll be able to light you.

REGINALD. What about the make up for us — like dad?

DICK. You don't need it. I want you fresh faced like kids should be.

REGINALD. We ain't kids. We're seasoned film stars now.

CHRISTINE. Definitely. *(grand)* And we want film star treatment.

REGINALD. A Cadillac convertible.

CHRISTINE. A black maid.

REGINALD. A penthouse.

CHRISTINE. A heart shaped swimming pool.

REGINALD. A luxury yacht.

CHRISTINE. One thousand pounds a week.

REGINALD. Two thousand.

CHRISTINE. Three.

REGINALD. Four.

CHRISTINE. Why haggle over money, darling?

REGINALD. *(dropping his grand attitude)* Look mister. We ain't kidding. No make-up. No film.

CHRISTINE. 'sright. We've only got to say that you're only conning 'im along to stay in the 'ouse, and 'e'll throw yer out.

DICK. *(insouciant)* Dearest children. You really are in a very weak position for blackmail. If I tell Mister Collier that I didn't invent any game to put you in the mood for acting, and that the confessions of murdering him came unaided from your sibling lips, what do you think would happen? I'd get thrown out, but you'd get something much more brutal. I dare say. *(suddenly hard, and cold)* So, shut up: do precisely as you're told, and there's an outside chance I won't say a dickie bird. An' I mean an outside chance! Because frankly I, and everybody else round here are fed up to the coccyx with the pair of you, and it wouldn't take much for me to land you both dead in the center of the vichysoisse. So prenez-garde, my little cherubs. Prenez bloody good garde, and take your positions on that frigging floor.

(The LIGHTS come up. Suddenly cowed and apprehensive, the children take up the indicated positions on the floor.)

DICK. Mrs. Collier, would you sit in for us please? *(MRS. COLLIER takes her position in the chair above the children. DICK sits on the dolly and looks through the camera. To BERNIE:)* Slowly back, Bernie. *(BERNIE pulls the dolly back as DICK tilts the camera down to frame the children.)* Hold it ... A fraction in. *(BERNIE pushes the dolly in a few inches.)* That's it. That's your final position. You'll track on my signal. *(BERNIE marks his position and the relight continues as DICK rejoins PHILIP. JOE fits the children with chest mikes.)* Well, I put the bite on the kids alright. They shouldn't give us any more trouble.

PHILIP. I heard you. It was most impressive. They look a happy little family now.

DICK. Happy families! I'm not at all sure I didn't prefer Master Slash and Miss Stab, the Killer Kids. God how I hate it. The ghastly genus familia commercium that we've all created.

ALEX. We're ready for you, Dick. *(The crew take up their positions as DICK and PHILIP walk over to "the set." PHILIP sits down in the chair facing MRS. COLLIER, while DICK takes a look through the camera.)*

PHILIP. Mrs. Collier, this really is the last time we're going to trouble you. All you will have to do is name your children for us, and if I ask you, agree with me that their hair looks good. OK?

MRS. COLLIER. Yes, alright. *(DICK comes off the dolly and his place is taken by ALEX.)*

DICK. All set, then. First Positions. Roll for a number!

ALEX. Camera rolling.

JOE. Sound running. Speed.

ALEX. Is this still version B sir?

DICK. Yes.

ALEX. Folliclean. Version B. Scene two. Take one. *(He claps the board and returns to the other side of the camera.)*

DICK. Action!

PHILIP. Now, Mrs. Collier, I see your children playing down there on the floor. Won't you introduce us to them? *(DICK makes a gesture and the camera is pulled back by BERNIE. ALEX tilts the camera down to frame the children as MRS. COLLIER speaks.)*

MRS. COLLIER. The older one is Reginald, he's fifteen. And the younger one is Christine. She's fourteen.

PHILIP. My word, their hair really does look clean and shiny, doesn't it?

MRS. COLLIER. Definitely. And we've had no more trouble with the dandruff neither.

PHILIP. Excellent. Reginald, why don't you tell us what you want to be when you grow up?

REGINALD. *(surly)* A racing driver.

PHILIP. And you, Christine, what do you want to be?

CHRISTINE. *(surly)* A model.

PHILIP. *(with heavy enthusiasm)* a racing driver and a model eh? Well, those are two glamourous professions alright. And of course they're both public ones too, so it's just as well that you have learnt the Folliclean habit early. From now on you and your mother can be sure that your hair will always be looking its best, thanks to Folliclean, the miracle hair shampoo, now with the new medicated additive HSA 590, to ensure our claim really works — that Folliclean, Cleans Follicles Cleanest of All.

DICK. Cut it. Check the gate. *(The camera is switched off. TED checks the gate as every one relaxes. BERNIE starts to chew on a sandwich.)*

PHILIP. Well, that was very good. Very good indeed.

MRS. COLLIER. Are we finished now then?

PHILIP. You are, Mrs. Collier. We'll hang onto the children for a few minutes longer if we may. Mr. Collier wants them to appear with him, in his spot.

ALEX. Gate's OK. *(MRS. COLLIER moves out of the lights taking off her chest mike. REGINALD and CHRISTINE rise from the floor.)*

DICK. Now then, Alex, what device would you suggest we use for Mr. Collier and the children — something formal, yet friendly?

ALEX. If we substitute the sofa for Mrs. Collier's armchair it will save us a major relight.

DICK. A suggestion of pure genius. If Bernie could bear to put that chippolata sandwich down for a moment, he could give us a hand. *(BERNIE puts down his huge sandiwch and comes over to help them shift the furniture.)*

BERNIE. It's not chippolata. It's liver sausage.

(The armchair is replaced by the sofa, as CLAIRE walks in.)

CLAIRE. He's all yours, Dick.

DICK. Come and sit in for Mr. Collier, will you, love. Great!

CLAIRE. *(Sits on the sofa.)* Always the stand-in. Never the star.

DICK. Reginald! Christine! Would you come over here, please? *(The children come across to sit beside him. He places REGINALD on right, and CHRISTINE on left.)* The boy is on the right. The girl is on the left. The boy is taller than the girl. Standard procedure!

ALEX. It should please Mr. Younghusband, at any rate.

DICK. Never let it be said that I failed to give a client the reassurance of an idea he's been exposed to a thousand times before. *(to ALEX:)* A medium shot moving to a tight three shot. Then we'll go in to a close up of dad, losing the kids. Right?

ALEX. Roger. *(ALEX and BERNIE work out and tape the three camera positions during this next dialogue between PHILIP and DICK. DICK moves into the "set" to check the set up. As he looks through the camera CLAIRE puts her arm round the children who resent it keenly.)*

CLAIRE. What a thing it is to have a loving father sitting amongst you chaps.

CHRISTINE. I'm a girl, if you don't mind.

ALEX. And what are you, Tiger? A murderer was it now? *(REGINALD shrugs the arm off violently and looks daggers at CLAIRE.)*

DICK. *(still looking through the camera)* The function of a stand-in, Claire, is to keep still. The same applies to you kids. *(to BERNIE:)* Right, now take me into the close position, pausing at your marks. *(BERNIE pushes the camera in to the first mark worked out by ALEX. DICK studies it for a moment.)* Good. *(The camera is then pushed into the second position. Again DICK studies it.)* Excellent, Alex. I couldn't have framed better myself. *(ALEX smiles and they swap places on the camera dolly which is drawn back to the first position. To PHILIP:)* Tell me something. I know why I'm making this commercial, I'm having a ball, but what about you? You know you can't use it, so why the hell are we bothering to do it? Why don't we just cut and run, right now?

PHILIP. Because if we did you can bet your bottom dollar that Mr. Collier would forbid his wife to sign the release form permitting us to use her performance on television.

DICK. Christ! I never thought of that.

PHILIP. A producer does have his uses sometimes. *(DICK freezes incredulously as BILL COLLIER Enters in full Sergeant Major's uniform. He is fairly heavily made up and is studying his reflection in a hand mirror. He is obviously fascinated by it.)*

CLAIRE. *(to BILL:)* How's that for a cheap winter tan, Mr. Collier?

BILL. Blimey! Is my face red? *(Laughs.)*

CLAIRE. Don't worry about it, Mr. Collier. All people appearing on television are made up the same color, otherwise they would tend to look as if they'd been recently dug up. *(CLAIRE immediately looks terribly embarrassed at her faux pas, but BILL COLLIER is too busy examining himself to have heard.)*

BILL. The boys wouldn't 'ave 'arf laughed to see me like this — with powder all over me face. Not that it isn't most becoming, of course. *(He continues to examine himself, fascinated with his own image.)*

CLAIRE. Surely you're not embarrassed Mr. Collier? *(Reluctantly BILL COLLIER puts the mirror down and moves down stage.)*

BILL. 'Course not! No more that is than a pregnant nun. *(Laughs.)*

DICK. Come along, Mr. Collier. We're ready for you now. Thank you, Claire. He looks fine. *(He leads BILL COLLIER over to the sofa. CLAIRE gets up and BILL COLLIER takes his place between the children. He is all smiles and joviality and puts his arms around their shoulders. They make no attempt to remove them.)*

BILL. *(to the children:)* Well, we're all stars together now eh? I'll show you I can playact with the best of you when I'm in the humor for it. Sir Laurence move over. *(Laughs. JOE comes forward with his chest mikes and proceeds to fit one round BILL COLLIER.)*

JOE. We'll just conceal this under your jacket, sir. Thank you. And the cord under your collar. That's it ... Just speak normal. You don't have to raise your voice or shout. *(PHILIP takes his place in his armchair with half profile to camera. JOE returns to his tape recorder.)*

PHILIP. Now Mr. Collier it's all quite simple. I'm going to ask you to tell me your story of how you and your family came to use Folliclean for the first time. I shall then go on to ask you further questions about the shampoo, questions relating to regular use and the subsequent health of the hair. Alright?

BILL. Right you are!

JOE. Speak for a level.

PHILIP. You are an ex-army man, Mr. Collier. When you were in the services did they give you anything to look after your hair with?

BILL. When I joined up, the regulation issue was saddle soap — men and horses for the use of. Mind you, things 'ave changed in the modern army. I h'understand in the new barracks they 'ave h'electric points by every bed for the lads' hair curlers. *(Laughs.)* I mean to say — you don't want it 'anging loose down their back do yer?

JOE. O.K. for sound.

DICK. Stand by. Alright, Philip?

PHILIP. Fine.

DICK. Now, Mr. Collier, I want you to keep everything nice and relaxed. Be as natural as possible, and whatever you do, don't look at the camera. The same thing of course applies to you children. Just keep smiling away at your father and you'll be alright. Do I make myself plain?

BILL, REGINALD, CHRISTINE. Right you are. Yes. Yes.

DICK. Right. Bernie, watch for my signal.

BERNIE. O.K., sir.

DICK. Turn over.

ALEX. Speed! *(ALEX comes out and holds the clapperboard up to the camera.)*

JOE. Sound running.

ALEX. Speed! Folliclean. Alternative Mr. Collier version. Scene One. Take One. *(He claps the board and returns to the other side of the camera.)*

DICK. Action!

PHILIP. Now, Mr. Collier. I understand that you and your family are all regular users of Folliclean.

BILL. That is correct.

PHILIP. Could you tell us how you came to use it in the first place?

BILL. Certainly. Me and the family was down at Westcliff on 'oliday. I remember it was a brisk day — no good for lying about in on the sands with nothing on, so I had the kids on parade ... There's nothing like a spot of drill to keep them warm. They loved it — marching and wheeling and doubling abaht, and very smart they looked I can tell you. No other kids to touch them on that esplanade.

(The camera starts to track in very slowly, on a signal from DICK.) Florie had cut down a couple of battle dresses she'd got from the army surplus to make them uniforms and I'd managed to scrounge them a couple of forage caps — no badges or insignia, naturally.

PHILIP. Mr. Collier. I don't quite see what this drill and the uniforms has to do with Folliclean. *(On a further signal from DICK the camera moves to its final position.)*

BILL. You don't, don't yer? Well I'll tell yer. It's got everything to do with it. Every perishing thing. I expect my squad to be alert and smart. Boots boned like mirrors; creases so sharp you can cut yourself; buttons that blind yer to look at them. Well on this day in question these kids was doing the slow march — a very h'impressive ceremonial maneuvre when h'executed correctly — and I 'appened to notice young Reginald's collar. Covered in dandruff it was. A thoroughly nasty sight! You remember, Reginald? I told you at the time — no soldier should be seen on parade in such a state.

REGINALD. *(parody of sergeant major's voice)* You there! You slovenly baboon's spawn you! What is that disgusting h'excrement you 'ave on your collar? *(BILL COLLIER, surprised at the interruption, gives REGINALD a furious look, which he immediately attempts to disguise with a laugh.)*

BILL. Now Reginald! Show more respect. No decent N.C.O. would h'address his detail in such a manner. *(to PHILIP:)* However, I did mention to his mother that I didn't exp'ect to see his uniform in that condition again, and she went straight up off the esplanade and bought a bottle of Folliclean at the chemist in the High Street. We didn't 'ave no more trouble after that.

PHILIP. *(unbelievingly)* And that's how the whole family started using Folliclean?

BILL. H'absolutely. I issued an order that it was to be used at least once a week, during morning h'ablutions.

PHILIP. *(weakly)* Thank you, Mr. Collier.

DICK. Cut it. Check the gate. Was that alright for you, Alex?

ALEX. Spot on. *(ALEX checks the gate. He does a pantomime of pretending to find a hair.)*

ALEX. *(serious)* TCH! Tch! Tch! *(Smiles.)* Gate's O.K. Is it a wrap, sir?

DICK. Yes, that's it.

ALEX. It's a wrap, boys.

DICK. Thank you, Mr. Collier — that was fine.

BILL. That's it then, is it?

DICK. That's it as far as I'm concerned, unless of course, Philip, you would like me to film a demonstration of the children, drilling outside in the street, to intercut with Dad's graphic narrative. I'm sure we could easily find a domestic pet in the neighborhood, to act as regimental mascot, and perhaps Mrs. Collier would be gracious enough to take the salute, and the kids could goosestep by, holding up bottles of Folliclean...

PHILIP. *(hurriedly)* I'm quite happy with what I've got, already, thank you all the same, Dick. And thank you, Mr. Collier. *(PHILIP rises and walks dazedly away.)*

BILL. Nothing to it then, is there, really. *(Gets up off the sofa.)* I could use a beer. I'm as dry as a... *(He goes over to the table and pours himself a beer. He offers a glass to Dick. The unit start dismantling the lights, camera and tracks, which they carry outside. They work very quickly and the room is soon put to rights. The children rise and hand their chest mikes to JOE.)*

DICK. *(to PHILIP while MR. COLLIER pours the beer:)* You sure you don't want to show it to Lionel? It's time he saw what real family feeling was actually about.

PHILIP. The man's a complete nut.

DICK. Not so fast. There might be other goodies in this house we haven't investigated. Don't you think it's odds on that there's some homicidal relative tucked away in the attic, or perhaps a scalping great-aunt whose dexterity with the tomahawk is the shameful secret of half Plaistow.

PHILIP. Oh shut up and let's move.

BILL. Just one moment, Mr. Charles.

PHILIP. Oh yes, before I go I'd like to leave you with a sample of the product just to tide you over until your year's supply arrives. *(He hands over the bottle he has been using in the commercial. MR. COLLIER looks at it suspiciously then puts it on the table.)*

BILL. I'm not worried about the year's supply, Mr. Charles. But what about the hundred nicker? I'd like to see the color of that before you shove off. Not that I don't trust you, mind, but...

PHILIP. Claire! There's a small matter of paying these good people. *(CLAIRE produces a wallet and two forms. She counts out two piles of twenty five pound notes.)*

CLAIRE. One, two, three, four, five. One, two, three, four, five. *(She gives one pile to MRS. COLLIER.)* There you are, Mrs. Collier. That's for all your hard work. *(MRS. COLLIER looks doubtfully at her husband.)*

BILL. Go on Florie, take it. It won't bite you. It'll come in handy for that new coat you've been wanting. *(MRS. COLLIER takes the money.)*

MRS. COLLIER. Well, thank you very much, I'm sure.

CLAIRE. Thank *you*, Mrs. Collier. And this is for your husband. *(She gives BILL COLLIER his hundred pounds.)*

BILL. Much obliged.

CLAIRE. If you both will just sign these release forms.

MRS. COLLIER. Oh, yes. *(She signs.)*

BILL. What are they?

CLAIRE. Merely a receipt for the money and your permission for us to use your performance on television...

BILL. Oh. Now we know then. My old woman would sign her own death warrant without reading it. *(He laughs indulgently and signs.)*

CLAIRE. Thank you. *(The room has been cleared of equipment and set to rights. JOE and BERNIE are all set to leave.)*

BERNIE. All clear, Alex.

ALEX. Fine. Well, get everyone in the coach. *(The two men head for the front door.)*

BERNIE. I'm going to miss this family.

JOE. You're on your own there, mate. *(Their voices die away. ALEX goes over to DICK.)*

ALEX. Wrapped up, sir.

DICK. Right. Move the unit off. We've got our own cars.

ALEX. Fine. See you back. 'Bye all.

MRS. COLLIER. Goodbye. *(ALEX goes out through the front door.)*

PHILIP. Well, we must be going. Goodbye, Mrs. Collier. You see the ordeal wasn't too bad, was it?

MRS. COLLIER. Oh, no. Not once you'd got the hang of it.

CHRISTINE. When will it be shown on telly, mister?

PHILIP. In about two months' time. Keep your eyes open for it.

REGINALD. Which one are you going to use?

PHILIP. Er ... it rather depends on which fits in better with the rest of the stories.

BILL. Surely there is no dispute abaht which is the better story, Mr. Charles?

PHILIP. *(hesitant)* None whatsoever, Mr. Collier. Goodbye once again and thank you for all your co-
operation.

MRS. COLLIER. Goodbye, Mr. Charles. Thank you for
being so patient with me.

PHILIP. Not at all.

CLAIRE. *(warmly)* Goodbye, Mrs. Collier. I thought you
were super.

MRS. COLLIER. Oh, I dunno.

CLAIRE. Yes. Super! Real dreamy.

MRS. COLLIER. *(flattered)* Well, that's nice. *(CLAIRE
makes a movement to kiss MRS. COLLIER but thinks better
of it.)*

CLAIRE. *(calling to PHILIP)* You coming, Phil?

PHILIP. I'm right behind you. *(CLAIRE walks out quickly,
pointedly ignoring BILL COLLIER and the children.)*

DICK. *(aside to PHILIP as he walks across the room)* May my
testicles become as dried lentils if I ever set foot in this
house again. *(BILL COLLIER follows them across the room to
the door.)*

BILL. Ta-ra, then. Don't do anything I wouldn't do.

PHILIP. 'Bye all.

MRS. COLLIER. 'Bye. Goodbye, Mr. Richards.

DICK. Goodbye, Mrs. Collier, and thank you for a
splendid performance. Farewell dearest children. It's
been a privilege and a pleasure knowing you. And the
same goes for you, Mr. Collier. It was the most instruc-
tive day of my life, and I might say, the most enjoyable.
I've never met anyone quite as extraordinary as you and
your family. It's been a delight! An absolute gold-plated,

copper bottomed, gilt-edged delight! Mr. Collier, I must tell you, if only there were more families like yours in the world, my job would be not only bearable but actually ennobling! Goodbye and a million thanks. *(They go out. BILL COLLIER closes the door behind him. Slowly he turns to face his family. The regard him tensely. Suddenly, like a snake striking, he thrusts out his hand, palm upwards towards MRS. COLLIER. She opens her bag and hands him her hundred pounds. He puts the notes in his pockets. All the traces of hail-fellow-well-met have left his face. The sergeant major has taken over completely.)*

MRS. COLLIER. *(nervously)* It's getting dark. I don't like to see the evenings drawing in.

(From now until the end of the act the scene gets steadily DARKER as night draws on.)

BILL. So you've been playing games about killing dear old dad, have yer?

REGINALD. The man explained...

BILL. What? That load of cobblers about you escaping from a Nazi prison camp. You h'escaped from your bedroom. That's what. And how did I know that? Because I h'ordered your mother to lock you in there this morning. You seem to 'ave forgotten that.

CHRISTINE. Well all the rest was true — about hiding you in the barn...

BILL. Don't provoke me, you lying little slut. You'll get a hiding, and it won't be in no barn, if I get my rag up. *(to MRS. COLLIER:)* You! Perhaps you would care to explain why, in spite of my h'express orders to the contrary, you let Reginald out of his room.

MRS. COLLIER. I couldn't help it, Bill. Honest I couldn't.

BILL. *(derisively)* You couldn't 'elp it. You couldn't 'elp yourself to your own dinner! I suppose you're going to tell me that some supernatural being glided up them stairs, and turned the bleeding key in the bleeding lock.

MRS. COLLIER. It was that television woman, Bill. They 'eard Reggie in the bedroom and sent her up to find out who were making the noise. She let 'im out.

BILL. Oh it was 'er, was it? ... Right now, you've got a spot of explaining to do, my little sly boots. You've been plotting this for weeks. Why didn't you tell me the people from the television was coming?

MRS. COLLIER. I thought you wouldn't let me 'ave them in the 'ouse, if I did.

BILL. *(sarcastic)* Why shouldn't I? We're the ideal family, are we not? Wife deceiving 'er model, 'ard working 'usband. Kids playing murder-me-dad. Ideal, eh? And what's more we all got rid of that nasty disease of the scalp as what everyone in England will shortly know we 'ad, didn't we? Well, didn't we? *(Silence. They don't look at him.)* Lost your tongues. Right then! Quite h'obviously what you need are some moments of contemplation which will 'elp you find 'em. Take your shoes off Christine. Reginald and Christine! Form up here! *(REGINALD and CHRISTINE move together.)* Attention! *(They come to attention.)* I find the charges of infamous conduct proved against both of you. You are therefore each sentenced to one month's solitary confinement in your bedrooms. You will leave them only to use the latrines at 0-600 hours and 1800 hours. Your mother will escort you on these journeys but you are forbidden to speak to 'er, on pain of further confinement. Your rations will be eight ounces of bread, a pinch of salt and a half pint of drinking water per day, except on Sundays when you will receive in h'addition one slice of meat and two h'ounces of a green vegetable. Is that understood? *(The children nod their heads.)*

MRS. COLLIER. *(distraught)* No, Bill! You can't do it.

BILL. Since when do you give the h'orders round 'ere, madam?

MRS. COLLIER. But Bill, what about... what about their school? They'll send someone to find out why they're not there.

BILL. Then you'll tell them they're being learnt at 'ome, not to be 'oly little liar brats, and not to invent games which 'ave as their h'objective the murderous destruction of those set over them.

MRS. COLLIER. But not a month, Bill. Not a month. A day. A few days. A week at the most. After all, they was only playing a game.

BILL. A game you call it? A flaming game? Well then, my girl, if — it's games you want, games you shall 'ave. And if it's telly commercials you want, telly commercials you shall 'ave. You there, Reginald, stand there at the table. *(barking)* Move! *(REGINALD marches to the table, and stands beside it.)* You Christine. On the floor, by this chair, kneel! *(CHRISTINE kneels on the floor.)* And you Florie, come and give me a hand. Now I shall be gone a few moments and while I'm away I want total silence. Not a word! Not a movement! I want to be able to 'ear a fly land on that ceiling. Understand? Right? *(He leaves the room and goes into the kitchen. MRS. COLLIER, head lowered, follows him.*

REGINALD and CHRISTINE remain as placed in total silence. They don't even look at one another. After a substanial pause MR. and MRS. COLLIER return. He is carrying a washing up liquid and a floor polisher. She is carrying a plastic bowl of water which she places on the table.) Now the dishes, Florie. And don't forget the cutlery. *(She goes out to the kitchen. BILL reads.)* Introducing Crackle! The all new washing up liquid. Just one drop gets all your dishes diamond bright, and sparkling clean, clean, clean. Well, Reginald, my lucky lad, you've seen it work on telly — here's your big chance to prove to yourself that it works in the privacy of your own 'ome. *(MRS. COLLIER returns with a pile of dirty dishes and cutlery which she sets down on the table. BILL COLLIER elaborately measures out exactly one drop of the liquid into the plastic bowl of water.)* There we are then. One pile of dirty dishes that your poor tired mother 'as thoughtfully left, and one bowl of common or garden water to which one whole drop of Crackle 'as been added. *(He cuts a very small piece of cloth into two tiny halves with a pair of scissors. He gives one of the halves to REGINALD.)* Now with the aid of this regulation issue cloth, washing up for the use of, let's see you get those dishes diamond bright, and sparkling clean, clean, clean. Detail! Commence cleaning operation now! *(REGINALD frantically tries to wash the dishes with his grossly inadequate equipment. BILL watches him for a moment, then turns his attention to CHRISTINE.)* Now then, it's your turn, my lucky miss. For you Christine, we 'ave *(reading)* Glitter — the wonder floor cleanser which shines and scents as it polishes. Makes your floors glass bright and cottage fresh in 'arf the time. *(He pours a little Glitter on the linoleum from the height he is standing and throws*

CHRISTINE the other tiny half of the rag he gave to REGINALD.) There's your up to the minute, with it, way out, h'equipment as h'advertised on T.V. All you need is the h'elbow grease — a first-rate product as what you won't see h'advertised on T.V. Right then ... Commence polishing operation now! *(CHRISTINE starts to polish the floor furiously. BILL COLLIER marches from one child to the other, inspecting their work, but talking to himself, gradually working himself up into a state of near hysteria.)* Come on lads put your backs into it! Faster! Faster! You won't get nothing clean if you're afraid of it. I've never seen such a stinking, depraved, bed wetting, gormless, idle lot in all my life. Yes, idle! You're too flaming idle to scratch your backsides when they itch. And you're too flaming ignorant to show proper respect to your superior h'officers. But I'll make decent soldiers of you lot yet, if I 'ave to break your 'earts in little pieces — if I 'ave to go on at you till you can't stammer nothing but yyess sssir, nnno sssir, you've got no sense of discipline — no sense of self-respect. You'd screw your own mothers to save yourselves the price of a whore. *(Suddenly, dazed, he realizes he has let himself get completely out of control. He pauses and picks up the plate REGINALD has been washing.)* Call that sparkling clean, clean, clean? It's as filthy as a grease monkey's jock strap? *(He drops it to the floor where it breaks. He moves over to where CHRISTINE is kneeling, polishing the floor.)* Call that looking-glass bright, and cottage fresh? It looks like a baboon's fouled the floor. *(He dirties it with his shoe. There is complete silence. The children don't move. BILL COLLIER wins his fight to control himself.)* Right! Detail atten-shun! Cleansing equipment, plates and cutlery, to the kitchen, at the double!

Move! One two. One two. One two ... *(The children double to the kitchen — REGINALD carrying the plates and cutlery. CHRISTINE with the rags and containers of Crackle and Glitter. They are out of the room a little time, and BILL grows impatient.)* Come on then you lot. Back here. No skyving. *(The children double back into the room and proceed to double on the spot until they hear the word of command.)* Detail halt! At ease! Stand easy! Atten-shun! To your rooms immediately — dis-miss! *(The children come to attention, turn to their right and march off up the stairs to their bedrooms. On the way, they pass their mother who makes a placating gesture. BILL COLLIER takes his coat off and sits down at the table and starts to read the evening newspaper.)* I'll 'ave me Scotch now, Florie. I need it.

MRS. COLLIER. Bill?

BILL. *(reading)* H'm?

MRS. COLLIER. I wish you wouldn't treat the kids like that. It ain't right.

BILL. It ain't right? Playing their filthy games. Playing at killing their dad.

MRS. COLLIER. Oh, Bill. Can't you see they only play them games 'cos they're unhappy? You never give them nothing but 'arsh words, and 'ard things to do. They're only kids when all's said and done...

BILL. Lying, skyving kids.

MRS. COLLIER. They can't be expected to like being tortured.

BILL. Tortured? I never...

MRS. COLLIER. All that army stuff. All that marching 'em abaht. Children must play...

BILL. It's for their own good. There's not an ounce of

discipline among the pair of them.

MRS. COLLIER. *(flaring)* You mean it's for your own good. You're the one what enjoys it.

BILL. Florie!

MRS. COLLIER. It's true, Bill. I knew you was a hard man when I married you. But a woman's different from kids. A woman can respect a man like you, but kids need a bit of fun. They need...

BILL. That's enough, Florie! I've 'eard enough. Where's me drink? *(MRS. COLLIER crosses slowly to the kitchen door.)*

MRS. COLLIER. Well I think it's a crying shame.

BILL. Do yer? Well just you remember *I* run things in this 'ouse.

MRS. COLLIER. *(Yells.)* Barracks you mean! *(She goes through to the kitchen. BILL COLLIER settles in his chair with an elaborate sigh of contentment. MRS. COLLIER returns with a three-quarter full bottle of whisky and a glass which she puts on the table. He uncorks it, and pours himself a large measure, and swallows half at a gulp.)*

BILL. That's better. *(He drinks the other half of his glass and pours himself another. A pause.)*

MRS. COLLIER. I told that T.V. chap abaht going to that funeral in my blue. I wonder if I did right.

BILL. Watcha mean?

MRS. COLLIER. I didn't tell 'im it was the funeral of my first 'usband.

BILL. Probably just as well. What did you tell him abaht a funeral for at all?

MRS. COLLIER. I 'ad to. It was me story. Reginald told 'im it was his dad's funeral but he didn't believe 'im.

BILL. I don't blame 'im. All that stuff abaht the kids killing me. He must have been pretty cheesed off and no mistake.

MRS. COLLIER. *(slowly)* They didn't say they 'ad killed *you*, Bill. They said they 'ad killed *their father.*

BILL. Well, I mean to say ... they *call me* dad. I've got into the 'abit of thinking...

MRS. COLLIER. Well there you are, then. But they was talking abaht their father. And I went to his funeral in my blue, see 'cos I couldn't wear my black on account of the dandruff...

BILL. Yes. Yes. But why should they say they killed 'im? What sort of a bombhead game is that?

MRS. COLLIER. 'e were a strict man with 'em, was Charlie — like you. Only 'e didn't make them do soldiers or anything. 'E was more like a schoolmaster, really. You know — trying to learn them to better their minds. I suppose it's difficult for kids to realize what's being done for them.

BILL. For God's sake, Florie, can't you answer a simple question?

MRS. COLLIER. They're good kids. *(MRS. COLLIER averts her face.)*

BILL. *(suddenly shouting at the top of his lungs)* Why did they say they'd killed their dad?

MRS. COLLIER. *(slowly and simply)* Because they did.

BILL. *(in horror)* They what?

MRS. COLLIER. I don't know quite 'ow it 'appened — they tell so many stories abaht it — always different, but they did it between them. One of them — Christine, I think hit 'im over the 'ead and Reginald 'eld 'im under the water. When I arrived I tried to revive 'im but it was too late.

BILL. *(excited)* Florie! Are you *actually* saying those kids of yours...

MRS. COLLIER. I'm sorry, Bill.

BILL. Are you round the twist or something? What about the police?

MRS. COLLIER. Well, there was no trouble there. They believed he'd dived off a rock, hit 'is 'ead and drowned.

BILL. I'm not talking abaht Charlie. I'm talking abaht the kids.

MRS. COLLIER. What abaht the kids? I could 'ardly give up me own children, could I?

BILL. They ought to be locked up. *(aghast)* The murdering devils!

MRS. COLLIER. Don't take on, Bill. If they was locked up, there'd be no one to look after them, would there?

BILL. What abaht Charlie? Did you spare a thought for him?

MRS. COLLIER. 'e were dead, weren't 'e? Besides 'e were no good for them. Always on at them — bullying them with questions they didn't know the answers to, and that sort of thing.

BILL. You can't go round murdering people for asking you questions.

MRS. COLLIER. They did.

BILL. This is insane. Why didn't you ever tell me?

MRS. COLLIER. If I'd told you Bill — you'd never 'ave married me.

BILL. You're dead flaming right, my girl. I'd never 'ave come within a mile of 'ere.

MRS. COLLIER. Well, there you are then. With kids like that I 'ad to 'ave a strong 'usband. The only trouble was 'e 'ad to turn out as big a bastard as the first one.

BILL. How dare you h'address me like that. You apologize this minute.

MRS. COLLIER. I'm sorry yer don't like it, Bill. But it's the truth. What those kids need is love, and looking after. Not being made to feel like worms no one wants, always. The way you're going with them two, you're asking for trouble.

BILL. Are you telling me that what they did to their father, they wouldn't 'esitate to do to their stepfather?

(BILL COLLIER suddenly stands up gasping. He loosens his collar and then hit by another fierce spasm, doubles up fighting for air. CHRISTINE and REGINALD steal silently down the staircase like animals emerging from a forest. They watch BILL COLLIER'S death throes dispassionately.)

REGINALD. Precisely.

CHRISTINE. You have it in one — Bill.

BILL. What's going on? I can't breathe. What 'ave you murdering little animals done to me?

REGINALD. Twenty milligrams in the whiskey bottle.

CHRISTINE. Alkaloid Nicotinana Tabacum, imported from the school laboratory some time ago.

REGINALD. A few seconds and the respiratory system is paralyzed.

CHRISTINE. And then pouff-bang! Heart failure!

REGINALD. Symptoms indistinguishable from alcoholic poisoning.

CHRISTINE. Unless you happen to apply the Stas-Otto process.

REGINALD. Which they won't in this case, because everyone knows poor old Bill liked his whiskey.

CHRISTINE. And so all you have to do, Mother, is tell the cops he was a boozer. O.K.? *(BILL COLLIER'S struggles grow suddenly weak and fitful.)*

REGINALD. Farewell Sergeant Major Bill Collier.

CHRISTINE. A great warrior, and an intrepid leather salesman. *(REGINALD mimes a trumpet player and hums the notes of the last post. BILL COLLIER, twitches, sighs in pain, and dies.)*

MRS. COLLIER. *(horrified)* My God. Not again. You haven't killed again.

REGINALD. Don't worry, Mother. There won't be no trouble.

MRS. COLLIER. Trouble. Of course, there'll be trouble. The police. The coroner ... I can't stand it all again.

REGINALD. The police won't come in to it. It will be death from natural causes. Just remember 'e was a boozy old bugger.

MRS. COLLIER. Reginald!

CHRISTINE. *(to REGINALD:)* Show some respect. You *are* in the presence of a man who will never eat another individual frozen television dinner ever again.

MRS. COLLIER. Christine! This is no joking matter. We're in grave trouble. All of us. And to think I was just warning 'im when it 'appened.

(There is a loud KNOCK on the front door. They all freeze.)

CHRISTINE. Quick! Into the armchair with him.

(Together they lift BILL COLLIER'S body into the armchair. The knocking is repeated.)

MRS. COLLIER. Just coming.
CHRISTINE. Cover his face.

(REGINALD takes the dead man's breast pocket handkerchief out of his pocket. He unfolds it, and delicately covers his face with it. He then arranges the limbs in a natural attitude of repose. Mother and son stare at one another. The KNOCK sounds again. MRS. COLLIER goes and opens the door. DICK stands outside.)

DICK. Surprise! Surprise! Here I am again. I'm sorry to disturb you but we're missing one chest mike. May I? *(He comes into the room, pushing past MRS. COLLIER and starts looking about him.)* It's around here somewhere. *(Suddenly he sees the body of BILL COLLIER with the handkerchief on his face. He addresses the children.)* Oh, dad's having a snooze, is he? It must be all that marching about he does.
REGINALD. *(suddenly blurting it out)* Having a snooze indeed. He's dead. I killed him.
DICK. *(wearily)* Oh, not again.
REGINALD. It's true. I poured the poison in his whiskey and shook it up so it would dissolve.
CHRISTINE. You rotten little liar. I did the whole thing. I stole the stuff from the lab. I put it in the whiskey.

REGINALD. You didn't.

CHRISTINE. I did. You wouldn't have had the guts.

REGINALD. *(to DICK:)* You don't believe her do you?

DICK. *(lightly)* Why not? Poison's a woman's weapon isn't it?

REGINALD. Men use it, too. It worked a treat, mister. He died horribly.

DICK. Good. Well that's two murders you've got away with kids. Congratulations. *(DICK resumes his search for the chest mike.)*

CHRISTINE. You don't believe us do you? *(Silence. DICK tries to laugh it off but he is getting involved in spite of himself.)*

DICK. Of course I do.

REGINALD. Well then, have a drink.

DICK. Oh yes, please.

MRS. COLLIER. No! That's your father's whiskey.

CHRISTINE. Well, why not take a look at him, then? I can assure you he's as dead as an Oxo cube and all twisted up with pain. *(Reluctantly, half curiously DICK goes over to BILL COLLIER'S body. Suddenly he sees the chest mike still round his neck.)*

DICK. I'm afraid I don't believe a word of your tiresome story, children, and you really ought to learn how juvenile it is to repeat a joke, but unfortunately I am going to have to wake your father anyway.

MRS. COLLIER. *(in panic)* Why?

DICK. The microphone's round his neck.

MRS. COLLIER. *(a desperate whisper)* Oh no!

DICK. I'm afraid so. *(Calls silently.)* Mr. Collier!

MRS. COLLIER. Couldn't you *please* come back some

other time? He's desperately tired.

DICK. This is a very valuable piece of equipment, Mrs. Collier. I'm sure he'll understand. *(calling louder)* Mr. Collier!

MRS. COLLIER. If you wake him he'll only take it out on me and the kids. Please! *(DICK suddenly catches sight of MRS. COLLIER'S agonized face.)*

DICK. Alright Mrs. C. Perhaps I can get it off without disturbing him. The cord's fairly loose. *(Very slowly and with infinite care DICK takes the microphone over MR. COLLIER'S head. Half way through the operation the body slips against DICK. He looks appealingly at MRS. COLLIER who moves quickly across to help. Slowly she pushes MR. COLLIER back into position as DICK finally removes the microphone.)*

MRS. COLLIER. *(soothingly to MR. COLLIER)* There, dear, it's alright. It's only one of the film gentlemen wanting his microphone back. You can go back to sleep now. *(DICK and MRS. COLLIER tiptoe away from the body towards the front door.)*

REGINALD. Aren't you even going to look at his face?

DICK. For the last time, no!

CHRISTINE. You don't know what you're missing.

DICK. *(firmly)* Goodbye, Mrs. Collier. You have my deepest sympathy.

MRS. COLLIER. Goodbye, Mr. Richards.

DICK. *(to the children:)* Goodbye you perfect murderers. Don't get caught now! *(He laughs and goes out, closing the door behind him. There is a short pause, then REGINALD and CHRISTINE burst out into hysterical giggling.)*

MRS. COLLIER. *(dully)* You won't laugh when they take

you away. Because I suppose you realize it's only a matter
of time before someone believes you, and they lock
you up.

REGINALD. They never *do* believe us, Mother. We're
only kids. And after all it's a thoroughly natural reaction.
all murderers want to boast about their crimes.

CHRISTINE. And go back to the scene of them. Let's go
to Tenby this summer.

MRS. COLLIER. I mean what I say. I can't protect you
against yourselves. *(sadly)* Perhaps in a way it would be a
good thing if it was all over.

REGINALD. *(tough)* You wouldn't turn us in, Mum,
would you? You wouldn't turn us in.

MRS. COLLIER. *(Shakes her head in bewilderment.)* No.

REGINALD. That's alright then. Isn't it? *(CHRISTINE
moves to sit beside her.)*

CHRISTINE. Don't worry Mum. Reggie's right about us
being kids. No adult ever really believes a child can speak
the truth about the adult world.

MRS. COLLIER. What do you mean — about the
adult world?

CHRISTINE. Killing is the adult world.

MRS. COLLIER. I only hope I can save you.

*(The TELEPHONE rings. They all look at each other. CHRIS-
TINE jumps up and answers it.)*

CHRISTINE. Hullo! Oh it's you, Mr. Younghusband.
Yes she's here. Hang on a moment. Mum, it's Mr.
Younghusband for you. (MRS. COLLIER takes the phone
from CHRISTINE.)

MRS. COLLIER. Hullo, Mr. Younghusband. What's that? *(pause)* Oh very well — Lionel. Beg pardon? No it's all finished. Everyone's gone ... No. Everyone's very pleased, I'm sure. What's that *(pause)* Next week? Well ... Well if you really want to I'm sure we'd love to ... Well, yes. Wednesday then. But are you quite sure? Alright, Lionel. I'll wait to hear from you. *(She replaces the receiver. To the children:)* That was Mr. Younghusband. He's asked us to 'ave dinner with him next week. Would my charming children like to meet his?

REGINALD. Whatever for?

CHRISTINE. He's after Mum, stupid.

REGINALD. The old goat.

MRS. COLLIER. That's quite enough of that! I think he's rather nice — a very sympathetic gentleman.

CHRISTINE. We'll have to get the funeral over before we meet Mr. Younghusband. Then everything'll be shipshape.

MRS. COLLIER. I don't know how I can face another funeral.

CHRISTINE. Just think how fetching you will look in your widow's weeds. *(affected voice)* "For years I couldn't wear my black, but now, thanks to Folliclean, I can attend my second husband's funeral with the assurance I lacked at my first." *(CHRISTINE fusses over her mother.)*

REGINALD. But don't worry. We'll always be with you to see you're happy, and that your man behaves decently.

CHRISTINE. That's right, Mother. That's what we're here for. *(a pause)*

REGINALD. I wonder if Mr. Younghusband will like us.

CHRISTINE. *(slowly)* He'd better! *(MRS. COLLIER raises her head and looks at her two children with dawning apprehension.)*

SLOW CURTAIN

Also by
Anthony Shaffer...

Murderer

Sleuth

This Savage Parade

Whodunnit

Please visit our website **samuelfrench.com** for complete
descriptions and licensing information.

OTHER TITLES AVAILABLE FROM SAMUEL FRENCH

WHODUNNIT

Anthony Shaffer

Mystery/Comedy / 7m, 3f / Interior

This Broadway success by the author of *Sleuth* takes audiences to
Agatha Christie's England. Six strangers and a butler have gathered
for a black tie dinner in a wealthy lawyer's mansion during a
thunderstorm. The guests include an aged rear admiral, a bitchy
aristocrat, a doddering old archeologist, a dashing young cad and
other Christie types. One of the guests is an oily Levantine who tells
the others (each in private) that he has the goods to blackmail them.
He is ripe for murder and so it happens. Whodunnit?

"A torrent of merriment ... heavy with excitement, crackles with
repartee, rings the bell with epigrams, and detonates depth charges
of laughter.... Converts the theatre into a discotheque of explosive
delight ... [with] enough riotous surprises to supply another mystery
dramatist with a trunkful of plays."
– *New York Magazine*

SAMUELFRENCH.COM

www.ingramcontent.com/pod-product-compliance
Lightning Source LLC
Chambersburg PA
CBHW070621120726
47909CB00004B/1273